THE FARNSLEY ASSIGNMENT

A Janet Markham Bennett Cozy Thriller

DIANA XARISSA

Copyright © 2022 DX Dunn, LLC

ISBN: 9798450667508
All Rights Reserved

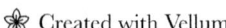 Created with Vellum

Chapter 1

"I'll go and get another round," Edward said. He stood up and then kissed Janet on the top of the head before walking away, heading for the bar that was in the next room.

Janet sat back in her seat in the dimly-lit back room of the New York City bar and smiled happily. Married life was turning out to be better than she'd ever imagined it would be.

"I'm terribly sorry, but hi," a voice said.

Janet jumped and then turned and looked at the pretty blonde at the next table. "Hi?" she replied questioningly.

The girl giggled. "Peter told me to leave you alone, but I couldn't resist saying hi."

"Hello," Janet said, smiling at the woman, who looked no more than twenty-five.

"Peter gets ever so annoyed with me when I start talking to strangers," the woman continued. "But I can't help myself. I love people, but more than that, I'm fascinated by them. I heard you and your husband, well, I assume he's your husband. I heard you talking, and I heard

1

your accents. You're British, aren't you? I wasn't one hundred per cent certain, because I sometimes mix up British accents with Australian ones, but I thought you sounded British. I asked Peter what he thought, and he said he thought I should mind my own business, but I said, 'What fun is that?'" The woman stopped and laughed loudly.

"We are British, and Edward is my husband," Janet replied when the laughter finally stopped.

"I knew it. I mean, I knew you were married. You act married, if that's a thing. I mean, it is a thing, because I could tell you were married. You just seem to belong together. I hope that Peter and I look the same way when we're together, but I'm not certain that we do. But maybe that's because we've only been married for a year. Maybe looking as if you belong together, maybe that's something that only happens after decades of being together. How long have you and your husband been married?"

Janet waited an extra second before she replied, not entirely certain that the woman was actually going to stop talking long enough for her to get a word in. "Edward and I got married in December," she said.

The woman blinked several times. "December? Last December? But it's only May, so you'd have only been married for, like, five months. That can't be right. You look as if you've been together forever. December of what year?"

Janet laughed. "Just last December, only five months or so ago. We've only known each other for a few years."

"Are you sure? I mean, of course you must be sure, but I'm just so confused. I was telling Peter, while we were watching you. Oh, but that sounds so creepy and odd, and it truly wasn't either of those things. But I was telling Peter that one day I want that to be us. I want us to just look as if we belong together. I want us to be able to sit and talk and still have things to talk about for years and years and years." She stopped and then frowned. "But you still have things to talk about because you've only been married for five months."

"But I'm sure you and Peter will be fine," Janet said quickly, wondering where the man in question was.

"Oh, I hope so. We've a lot to talk about at the moment, because we're thinking about having children. Do you have children? I mean, I suppose you don't have them with your new husband, but have you ever had children?"

"I've never had children of my own, but I did my best to touch as many young lives as possible. I was a primary school teacher for nearly forty years."

"Primary school? Is that like elementary school, or is it older kids? Isn't it weird how you have different words for things than we do in America? I mean, it's the same language, so why are so many of the words different? My brother dated a girl from Liverpool for a few weeks. She wasn't in Liverpool, she was here, well, not here in New York City, but here in the US. She was in Ohio, because that's where we were living at the time. Actually, we still live there, all except my brother, but that's beside the point. Where was I?"

Janet swallowed another laugh. "Your brother dated a girl from Liverpool."

"Yes, he did. She did a study abroad thing for a semester at the college he was attending, and they went out for a few weeks. She said all sorts of things he couldn't understand. That isn't why they broke up, though. They broke up because she didn't want to stay in Ohio forever. My brother did, then, but now he's in Wyoming, of all places. I don't think she would have liked Wyoming either, to be honest, but I think it's funny that they broke up because she didn't want to stay in Ohio, and now he isn't even in Ohio. Isn't that funny?"

Janet nodded. "I believe you're correct. Primary school is what you would call elementary school."

The woman stared at her for a moment and then nodded. "Oh, right, that's right. That's what we were talking about. You never had children, but you used to be a teacher. Did you quit teaching, then, when you got married? I would love to quit working now that I'm married. Women used to do that years and years ago, but no one does it these days. Some women do quit when they have children, but then the children take up all of their time and energy. I'm pretty sure they're more work than my job, even though I work very hard at my job."

"What do you do?" Janet asked.

"My sister and I have a little restaurant. It's more like a diner than a proper restaurant. It isn't fancy or anything. Carol, that's my sister, she's always been better at getting up early, so she goes in and gets everything set up and deals with the breakfast crowd, and then I go in around ten-thirty and help clean up breakfast and get things ready for lunch. After lunch, we shut for a few hours, and then we reopen from four until seven for dinner. My sister goes home around six most nights, since she came in early. I'm usually there until eight-thirty or nine, cleaning and getting everything ready for the next day. We're open six days a week, but we're shut on Mondays, which sounds odd, but weekends are our busiest time, and by Sunday night, we both need a day off."

"It sounds as if you work very hard indeed."

"Carol always says she works harder than I do, because she does most of the cooking, but I cook after six if anyone comes in once she's gone for the day, and I could cook all day long if she didn't want to do it, but she'd rather cook and I'd rather be out front, chatting with the customers."

It's a wonder anyone ever gets to leave, Janet thought, looking around to see what was keeping Edward.

"Peter is an electrician," the woman added. "We met when Carol and I first bought the restaurant. The building was in terrible condition, and besides patching up the walls and painting and putting in new flooring and a million other things I can't even remember, we had to have all new wiring put in throughout the entire building. Carol and I picked three different electricians out of the phone book and had them come to give us quotes. Peter's wasn't the least expensive, but he wrote on the bottom of the quote that he'd take ten per cent off if I'd have dinner with him." She laughed and then blushed. "I very nearly said no, actually."

"How long ago was that?"

"That was nearly four years ago. I'd just finished college with a degree in marketing. Carol has a degree in English, which isn't much help with the business, not that my marketing degree has done much for us, either, but that's neither here nor there."

"I have a business with my sister, too," Janet interjected.

"Really? I thought you said you were a teacher."

"I was a teacher for many years, but I took early retirement," Janet explained. "My sister and I had always lived together in a small cottage near the school where we taught. When she decided to retire, we did the maths and discovered that I could retire as well. We thought we'd spend our time reading and enjoying doing nothing much, while saving every spare penny for travelling."

"That sounds lovely. I wonder if Carol will want to see

the world with me once we're both ready to retire? But what about Edward? Where does he fit into the story?"

"I hadn't met Edward yet," Janet explained. "A short while after we retired, Joan and I were informed that we'd inherited a small sum of money from a distant relative."

"Joan is your sister?"

"My goodness, I'm doing this all wrong," Janet laughed. "Yes, Joan is my sister. I'm Janet Markham Bennett, by the way."

"And I'm Cara Hughes Hopkins," the woman replied. "We should have started there, really, shouldn't we? But now you have to keep going because things were just getting interesting. I'd love to suddenly inherit a fortune from a distant relative. Ideally, it would be someone that I've never met, so I wouldn't feel too sad that they'd died, but even if I didn't know them, it would still be very sad, wouldn't it? Inheritances are, by their very nature, sad things. Perhaps it would be best if I simply won the lottery. Peter laughs at me when I buy tickets, but I've allocated five dollars every week for lottery tickets. Those five dollars allow me to dream. When things are quiet at the restaurant, I try to imagine what I'm going to do when I win big. I could still do that, I suppose, even if I wasn't buying tickets, but it wouldn't feel the same if I knew that I couldn't possibly win."

Janet nodded slowly while she tried to remember what they'd been talking about before Cara's latest ramble. "Joan had always had a dream, actually," she told Cara. "She'd always wanted to own a bed and breakfast, but she'd never told me."

Cara made a face. "Why not? I share everything with my sister. Carol gets tired of hearing about all of my hopes and dreams. She tells me all the time to stop dreaming and start working harder, but I work plenty hard enough. She just doesn't have enough imagination."

"Joan had never told me because she'd never believed that owning a bed and breakfast would be possible," Janet said quickly, as the woman paused for a breath. "But once we'd inherited some money, the dream suddenly seemed feasible. I don't know that she would have actually done anything about it, really, if she hadn't seen the perfect bed and breakfast for sale near us, though."

"Oh? There's nothing better than good fortune and serendipity working together. Carol and I felt as if we'd had a bit of both when we first started talking about opening a restaurant together. We didn't find the perfect property, though. We found a terrible property and transformed it into the perfect property."

"I'm not certain either Joan or I could have managed that, but Doveby House in Doveby Dale in Derbyshire had already been turned into a bed and breakfast by its previous owner. When she died suddenly, she left the property to a local charity, and the charity was eager to sell quickly. They sold it to us fully furnished with gorgeous antiques and with a library full of books."

"So you own a bed and breakfast? How very European. I've only ever stayed in hotels, but then, I've never been to Europe. I don't often leave Ohio, really. I love it there, I really do, but travelling is exciting in all sorts of ways. Peter and I went to Niagara Falls for our honeymoon, but we stayed on the American side of the Falls. We weren't sure what we needed to go across into Canada. Neither of us has a passport. Do you need one to go to Canada? I'm sure you must need one to go to England, don't you?"

"Yes, you'd need a passport to visit England. I don't believe they're terribly expensive. Perhaps you and Peter should get them and then do a bit of European travel before you think about adding to your family."

"I don't know. Carol isn't very happy that I took a weekend off to come to New York. We're celebrating our first wedding anniversary, and she said she hopes I don't plan to celebrate all of them," Cara replied with a small laugh. "I think next year we may have to just have a nice dinner somewhere in town. But you still haven't told me how you met Edward."

"Ah, yes, Edward," Janet said, smiling as she remembered the first time she'd seen the man. "He knocked on our door just a short while after we'd purchased Doveby House. We weren't ready for guests yet, but he'd made a booking with the previous owner, and we couldn't turn him away."

Janet could only hope that she wasn't blushing too badly as she told the small lie. When Edward had arrived, he'd claimed that he'd had a previous booking, but she'd later learned that that wasn't true. Instead, he'd been sent by a top-secret government agency to search Doveby House. Under the previous owner, Edward's agency had sometimes used the property as a safe house, and Edward was there to make certain that no evidence of that had been left behind.

"And was it love at first sight?" Cara demanded. "Not that I believe in love at first sight. I didn't even like Peter when I met him. I didn't think he was all that attractive, and I thought it was a bit rude, offering us a discount if I went out with him. It felt all wrong, really, and I told Carol I wouldn't do it. Then Peter came back to see us with some sketches of what he wanted to do with the lighting. We'd only asked for estimates on what it would cost to have the building rewired, but he drew up all these gorgeous plans for all kinds of different lighting in the different parts of

The Farnsley Assignment

the restaurant and, well, I fell in love with his ideas, I suppose. Let's just say that I was impressed enough to agree to have dinner with him after that."

"I wasn't terribly fond of Edward when I first met him, either," Janet admitted. "He stayed with us for only a few days, but before he left, he told me that he was interested in getting to know me better. Then he more or less disappeared."

"Disappeared?"

Janet flushed. *If you aren't careful, you'll say something you shouldn't*, she told herself sternly. "He was meant to be retired, but he was still travelling a great deal for work. He used to ring me occasionally, and he sent me quite a few gifts as well, but we only saw one another very rarely."

"What sort of gifts? Peter is usually very good at finding me lovely things, but the first thing he ever gave me nearly ended our relationship. We'd only gone out twice, and I was starting to think that things were going well, and then he turned up at my house with this big stuffed teddy bear, and I nearly dumped him on the spot."

"You don't care for teddy bears?"

"Oh, no, I love Mr. Snuggles. That's what I call him. He's wonderful, but it was just too soon in our relationship for him to give me something like that." She shrugged and then laughed. "It sounds silly, but at the time I felt like he was rushing things in some way. The only reason I didn't end things, really, is because he didn't buy Mr. Snuggles for me."

Janet frowned as she waited for the rest of the story. Cara was unusually silent.

"What do you mean by that?" Janet finally asked.

"Oh, I mean he'd been given Mr. Snuggles, and he obviously didn't have any use for a giant teddy bear, so he thought he might as well give him to me. He'd been working at the local arcade, doing some electrical work for them, you see. While he'd been working on one of the machines, he'd triggered something, and it had spit out, like, a million tickets. When he took them to the manager and explained, the manager laughed and gave him Mr. Snuggles. Apparently, once the tickets were dispensed, it was easier for him to just give out a prize than to try to tell the system to void however many tickets had come out in error. If it had all happened a few months later, it wouldn't have mattered, anyway, because by then Peter's sister was pregnant, and he could have given her the teddy bear for the baby."

"Edward bought me a painting that I'd admired in a local shop," Janet said after she'd mentally rewound the conversation. "And he sent flowers quite regularly. He also had his sister bring me a kitten. When my sister and I had trouble with our car and had to borrow one from a local garage, I fell in love with the borrowed car, and Edward bought that for me as well."

"Wow, no one has ever bought me a car. No wonder you married him."

Janet laughed. "I didn't marry him because he bought me a car. I married him because he makes me happy."

"So, he finally retired?"

"He finally retired," Janet agreed. "And once he'd done that, he came to stay at Doveby House. Joan had just recently married the widower who lived across the road from us."

"She'd never been married before, either? So, you both found love after you'd retired? Maybe I was too hasty, getting married at twenty-four."

Janet shook her head. "You should get married when you find the person with whom you want to spend the rest of your life, whenever that happens."

"So, what brought you and Edward to New York?" Cara asked.

Careful, careful, Janet thought. "We're doing some travelling," she said vaguely. "Edward used to come here for work quite a lot, so he wanted to show me the city."

"What do you think of it?"

"I don't have much experience with big cities, but I'm enjoying being here. We spent some time in London before we came here, and I'm fascinated by the differences and the similarities between the cities."

"It's crazy at the bar," a young man said as he put two glasses on the table where Cara was sitting.

Janet smiled at the man, who had brown hair and green eyes. He wasn't the handsomest man she'd ever seen, but when he looked at Cara, his eyes lit up.

"This is Janet," Cara told him. "Janet, this is Peter, my husband."

Janet grinned at the pride in the woman's voice. *They might just make it to forever,* she thought. "It's very nice to meet you," she told Peter.

He laughed. "I suppose you know everything there is to know about me by now. Cara can't seem to help herself. She talks to everyone."

"We've had a lovely chat while we've been waiting for our respective husbands to return from the bar," Janet replied.

"It's a mess out there," Peter said. "There are only two bartenders, and one of them doesn't seem to know how to do much more than open beer bottles." He glanced at Cara. "You were lucky I got the other guy. He knew how to make your fancy drink."

Cara laughed and lifted her glass. "Cheers," she said. "I don't really drink very often, but when I do, I like fun fruity drinks."

Janet opened her mouth to reply but froze in her seat as Edward walked back into the room. He was frowning, and so were the men in black suits on either side of him.

"That's scary," Peter said. "Those guys look like hired muscle. I wonder what the old guy with them did to get himself into so much trouble."

"That's my husband," Janet said anxiously.

Chapter 2

"Darling, I'm afraid we're needed elsewhere," Edward said when he reached the table. His two companions remained in the doorway, staring straight ahead, with blank expressions on their faces.

"It was lovely meeting you," Janet said to Cara and Peter. "I hope you have a long and happy life together."

"Are you going to be okay?" Cara asked, putting a hand on Janet's arm.

Janet smiled at the woman. "Everything is fine," she assured her. "If you're ever in Derbyshire, you must visit me at Doveby House."

"Yes, of course we will," Cara replied.

Janet followed Edward towards the door, stopping before she reached it to give Cara a quick wave. Cara and Peter were both completely forgotten as she and Edward were ushered into a waiting taxi by the two men. They shut the door behind Janet, and she watched as they got into the taxi that had been parked behind theirs. A moment later, their car pulled into traffic with the other car right on its bumper.

"What's happening?" Janet demanded in a whisper.

"I'm not entirely certain," was Edward's unsatisfactory reply. "We'll find out soon enough, though. For now, just sit back and relax."

All of the uncertainty made it impossible for Janet to relax, of course. She sat back and stared out the window for a moment, but she had too many questions to sit still for long.

"Are these the good guys or the bad guys?" she hissed.

Edward looked surprised, and then he pulled her into an awkward sideways hug. "I'm sorry, darling, I never thought that you might be surprised and concerned by what was happening. I would be behaving quite differently if we were in any danger," he assured her. "The men from the bar are American agents, sent by Chuck Hanson to find us. They did that as a courtesy to Mr. Jones, though. It's Mr. Jones who wants to speak to us."

Janet felt a rush of relief. That was quickly followed by a new set of fears. "What does Mr. Jones want? He's scary in his own way."

"I've absolutely no idea, but I think we're about to find out."

The car had pulled up in front of a large luxury hotel. When it stopped in front of the entrance, a uniformed hotel employee opened the door next to Janet.

"What happens if I run?" she asked Edward before she moved.

"I don't think you'd get far," he replied, nodding towards the two men in black who'd already climbed out of their taxi and were quickly approaching Janet and Edward's car.

Janet sighed and then let the man holding the door help her out of the car. "Thank you," she said.

"You're very welcome, Mrs. Bennett," he replied.

The Farnsley Assignment

Janet gasped, but Edward didn't seem at all bothered that the man knew her name. He'd followed her out of the car, and now he offered her his arm. She took it, and then the pair followed the two men in black into the hotel. They were escorted through the elegant lobby and down a short corridor. At the end of the hall, one of the men opened a door marked "Private" and gestured for them to walk through it.

Janet couldn't resist taking a good look around once she was through the door, as it was highly unlikely that she'd ever have another chance to see a private space in a luxury hotel again. She was disappointed as they continued down another long hallway that had clearly had far less money spent on it than what she'd seen on the other side of the door.

The carpet was an ugly brown that was stained and threadbare. The walls had been painted some sort of off-white shade that was now covered in fingerprints and scuff-marks. The two men stopped in front of the last door on the left. One of them knocked sharply and then, when a voice called "come in," he opened the door.

"In you go," he told Janet and Edward.

Janet hesitated. Edward squeezed her hand and then stepped in front of her and into the room. Janet followed. As she crossed the threshold, the man holding the door shut it behind her. She jumped as the door banged into place.

The room they'd entered was large and dimly lit. Edward took another step forwards and then stopped. Janet looked around at rows of shelves that held piles of sheets and towels.

"It's a storage room," Janet whispered.

Edward grinned at her. "It took me a minute to spot it. Come on." He led her across the room to the far wall. As they approached, a section of the wall suddenly slid sideways, revealing a large office space.

Janet gasped. "It's like something out of a movie," she said softly.

"We do what we can," a familiar voice boomed. "I doubt our British counterparts spend as much time and effort on such things, but there's nothing I love more than a hidden door or a secret entrance."

Chuck Hanson pulled Janet into a hug before she could reply. "How are you?" he asked as he released her.

"I'm fine," she replied. "Although I was more than a little anxious when I saw Edward surrounded by your men."

Chuck laughed. "Edward could have taken them both out in seconds if they'd been a threat to him. I've no doubt about that. I didn't mean to frighten you, though. Next time, I'll send one of my less-intimidating agents to track you down. I would have sent Karl if he were in the country, but unfortunately, he's in Bolivia at the moment."

"Bolivia?" Janet echoed.

"I can't say anything more than that," Chuck replied. "But come and sit down. Can I get you a drink?" He led them to a cluster of couches and chairs in one corner of the room.

Janet sat down and then exhaled, feeling as if she'd been holding her breath since she'd first spotted the two men with Edward.

"You prefer white wine, don't you?" Chuck asked.

"I think I'd rather not have anything alcoholic right now," Janet replied. "I'll wait until we hear about the assignment."

Chuck nodded. "That's very sensible. Mr. Jones suggested that there was some urgency, but he hasn't – ah, that will be him now," he said as a loud ringing noise made Janet jump.

"Let's see if I can make this work," Chuck said as he sat down next to Janet and Edward.

He picked up a remote control and began pushing buttons. After a moment, the large screen on the wall flickered to life. Janet stared as she recognised Mr. Jones looking back at her through the screen.

"Ah, is this working, then?" Chuck asked.

"I can see and hear you," Mr. Jones replied.

"And we can see and hear you," Chuck said. "Hurray for technology!"

Mr. Jones nodded. "Edward, Janet, thank you for agreeing to meet with me."

"That isn't exactly what happened," Janet muttered under her breath.

Edward took her hand and squeezed it tightly.

"I hope nothing is seriously wrong," Edward said.

"I know you've been enjoying your time in New York for the past month, but we have an assignment for you, if you're interested," Mr. Jones replied.

"I don't know. The last one was a bit of a mess," Edward replied.

"Yes, it was, at that," Mr. Jones agreed. "This one is something rather different."

"Oh?" Edward didn't sound especially interested.

"Arthur Farnsley has invited his only son, John, to visit him on his private island in the Bahamas this weekend. John will be joined by his wife, Sarah. Also invited for the weekend are John and Sarah's three children and their respective spouses. There will, of course, be servants in attendance as well," Mr. Jones told them.

"My days of acting as a butler are long gone," Edward said.

Chuck laughed, and Janet was certain she saw a hint of a smile pass over Mr. Jones's face for a fraction of a second.

"If you choose to join the party, you'll be attending as one of John's old school friends," Mr. Jones told him. "You and your lovely wife are hoping to fit in a short sail around the Bahamas before hurricane season begins. When you heard that John was going to be visiting his father's island, you suggested that you could sail over for a reunion."

"I assume we're sailing with a full crew," Edward said.

"Of course. You and your wife know next to nothing about sailing," Mr. Jones replied.

Edward nodded. "Which island?"

"Arthur calls it Farntopia. It has an official name, but all of that information is in the file," Mr. Jones replied.

"And why are we needed in Farntopia?" Edward asked.

Mr. Jones frowned. "Let's just say that it has been deemed desirable for someone from the agency to be there."

"Let's not," Edward countered. "What's really happening there? Or what do you suspect is happening? Or what do you think will happen once the whole family arrives?"

Mr. Jones sighed. "All of the information that I have available is in the file that you'll be given if you agree to the assignment. It isn't much, though."

"You never send agents into an assignment without a full understanding of what they are meant to be doing," Edward argued.

"This is an exceptional case," Mr. Jones told him. "The assignment has come directly from Smith, and you and Janet were specifically requested."

"Smith doesn't usually get involved at that level," Edward replied.

"I am aware of that," Mr. Jones replied tightly.

"So Smith has some connection to someone who will be staying at Farntopia this weekend," Edward said thoughtfully. "Who?"

"I have no further information," Mr. Jones said.

"In that case, I don't think we're interested," Edward replied. "We've no way to accurately determine the level of danger into which we may be putting ourselves. I think it's best if we decline this one."

"Janet, what do you think?" Mr. Jones asked.

Janet jumped. "Me? I've no idea. If Edward thinks it's a bad idea, I'll defer to him, because he has decades more experience than I do."

"Surely you'd appreciate spending a weekend on a private Bahamian island," Mr. Jones said.

"If that is something that Janet thinks she would enjoy, you know that I can arrange for an invitation elsewhere," Edward interjected.

Mr. Jones frowned. "Smith wouldn't be asking you to go if there weren't a reason for it."

"And I may agree, once I've heard the reason," Edward countered. "But until then, I'm not interested."

There was a long pause before Mr. Jones spoke again. "Smith suggested that you might consider the assignment as a personal favour."

Edward looked shocked. "A personal favour?" he echoed.

Mr. Jones nodded. "And a one-off event as well. I've been assured of that."

"I don't like it," Edward said.

"I don't like it, either," Mr. Jones admitted. "If it were up to me, I wouldn't be sending anyone on this assignment, let alone one of my best agents, but my orders come from above."

"From Smith," Edward said flatly.

"And elsewhere," Mr. Jones replied.

Edward raised an eyebrow. "Interesting."

Mr. Jones sighed. "If you are determined not to take the assignment, I need to get busy. I don't have much time to find a replacement."

Edward looked at Janet. "I don't know what to tell you," he said. "We'd be taking an assignment without knowing why we're being sent where we're being sent. It could be dangerous, or it could be nothing at all. There often isn't much in between those two in this business."

"Someone must be in danger," Janet speculated.

"Or something," Edward added. "Maybe Sarah is planning to wear the Farnsley diamond during the weekend, and we're being sent to guard the stone."

"Surely, if that were the case, we could be told everything," Janet argued.

Edward shrugged. "I would have thought so."

"If you'd rather, you can take the assignment on your own," Mr. Jones suggested. "Janet could remain in New York, and we could find someone to keep her company. I believe I could spare Christopher for the weekend."

Janet raised an eyebrow. Edward had worked under Mr. Jones's supervision for many years. Christopher had been hired much more recently as a sort of assistant to the older man. He was only in his mid-twenties, and Janet found him intelligent, charming, and kind. She very much enjoyed his company, and the thought of spending a weekend with him in New York appealed in some ways. That Mr. Jones had suggested it made the assignment in Farntopia seem more important.

"I'm not going without Janet," Edward said flatly.

"But are you going?" Mr. Jones asked.

Edward hesitated and then looked at Janet again. "Are we going?" he asked.

Janet shrugged. "It sounds as if it might be important."

"Yes, it does, which is worrying."

"I've never been to the Bahamas," Janet added.

Edward smiled at her. "It is lovely," he said. "And it will be warmer and sunnier than New York in May."

"Hurricane season doesn't start until June," Mr. Jones said. "You should have perfect weather."

Edward frowned, but then nodded slowly. "It's just for the weekend?" he asked.

"That's what I've been told," Mr. Jones replied. "The family will all be arriving tomorrow, starting with John and Sarah, who are expected to reach the island in the morning. You'll be welcome any time after midday."

"We need to get back to our flat and pack, then," Edward said.

Mr. Jones nodded. "Your flight leaves in three hours. You'll be flying into Nassau and boarding your yacht there. The yacht has a crew of three, who will accompany you to Farntopia and then leave you there."

"Leave us there?" Janet echoed.

"There isn't enough dock space for everyone. Your yacht will have to dock at one of the nearby islands," Mr. Jones explained. "The details are in the file that Chuck will provide."

"A little light reading," Edward muttered as Chuck handed them each an envelope.

"We'd better get moving," Janet said as she slipped her envelope into her large handbag.

"Thank you," Mr. Jones said. "I didn't want to have to ring Smith with bad news."

Janet thought for a moment that Mr. Jones looked frightened by the thought. She opened her mouth to speak, but the screen suddenly went blank.

"We're clear," Chuck said. "And now that I can't be

overheard, let's talk. Do you want me to send a few guys down to keep an eye on the situation?" he asked Edward.

Edward shook his head. "Whatever is happening is clearly complicated. I've worked for the agency for forty years, and I've never been asked to do any favours for Smith. We don't want to do anything that might raise suspicions anywhere."

"How about that drink now, then?" Chuck suggested.

Edward chuckled. "We need to focus on our assignment for now."

"In that case, I'll get you a ride back to your apartment," Chuck said. "A car will pick you up at your hotel at three to take you to the airport."

Janet glanced at her watch and then frowned. "That doesn't give us much time."

"It's the best I can do," Chuck countered.

Janet followed Edward and Chuck out of the room and then back down the corridor. He escorted them to a taxi and then waved as the taxi drove away.

"The Bahamas?" Janet said as they went. "I assume you've been there before."

Edward nodded. "I've been everywhere before," he told her.

Janet laughed. "Have you been to Farntopia before?"

"No, and I'm not certain I want to go this time," he replied with a frown. "But we're committed now."

"Maybe it will turn out to be nothing. The last case did, really."

"Lightning rarely strikes twice," Edward replied.

"My buddy, Phil, he got hit by lightning twice," the cab driver interjected. "The first time, he was just out walking, minding his own business, like, and then bam, boom, zzzzit, he was on the ground with steam coming out of his ears."

"My goodness," Janet said.

"The second time, he was playing golf, which everyone knows you shouldn't do in a thunderstorm, but he told everyone he was safe because he'd already been struck once before. That didn't stop the lightning from zapping him again, though. Boom, bash, wallop, he got knocked right off the tee."

"Gracious, I hope he was okay," Janet replied.

"He was fine," the cabbie assured her. "He limps a bit now, and he can't use his left arm properly, but otherwise, he's fine."

Janet looked at Edward, who was trying not to laugh.

"I would imagine he's a good deal more cautious in storms now," Janet said.

"Not at all," was the unexpected reply. "He reckons he must really be immune now, so he pays no attention whatsoever to storms. He can't properly golf, because of his arm, but he'll go and play putt-putt with his friends in all sorts of weather. Except no one will play with him anymore. We all figure he attracts lightning now."

Janet still hadn't worked out how to reply to him when the man pulled up in front of their building. Edward paid him as Janet got out of the car. A few minutes later, they were inside their luxury flat.

"What should I pack?" Janet asked.

"It's only a weekend," Edward replied. "And it's going to be hot and sunny. Shorts, T-shirts, swimsuits, that kind of thing."

"I haven't worn a swimsuit in decades."

"But now you live part of the year on a yacht. Women who do that wear swimsuits."

"I don't even own any swimsuits."

Edward nodded and then pulled out his mobile. He pushed a button and then spoke. "I need six to eight swimsuits for Janet, please," he said. After a moment, he looked at Janet. "Would you prefer any particular colour?"

"Black is slimming. But you can't just order up swimsuits in that way. You didn't even ask my size. Besides, I need to try them on. Swimsuits are horrible things to try to buy under any circumstances. You'll get me six and none of them will fit."

"They'll all fit," Edward assured her. "The agency has notes on what sizes you wear. Any special requests? Bikinis? One-piece? What would you prefer?"

"I've never worn a bikini, and I don't intend to start now," Janet told him. "I want modest styles that cover as much as possible. And a cover-up for when I'm not actually in the water."

"Matching cover-ups for each suit," Edward said into his phone. "As quickly as possible, please."

They walked together into the bedroom. While Janet opened the doors to the huge walk-in closet and began to search for things to pack, Edward pulled out two large suitcases. Half an hour later, Janet threw up her hands and sighed.

"That's the best I can do, aside from the swimsuits," she told Edward. "I think I have everything, but I'm certain I've forgotten at least one essential item."

He chuckled and then pulled her into a hug. "We aren't going to the ends of the Earth. There are shops in the Bahamas, and I suspect Farntopia is fully stocked with everything you could possibly need as well. We'll be fine."

"I hope so."

Edward was just zipping up the cases when someone knocked on the door. Janet opened it to a courier who was holding a large box.

"Janet Markham Bennett?" he asked.

She nodded, and he handed her the box. After signing for it, she carried it into the bedroom.

"Your swimsuits, I assume," Edward said.

Janet put the box on the bed and opened it. "There must be a dozen suits in here," she said. "And at least that many cover-ups as well."

"We don't have time to go through them now," Edward told her.

He picked up the box and dumped the entire contents into one of the suitcases. Janet had to help him hold it closed as he zipped it shut. He was still wheeling the cases towards the door when their house phone buzzed.

"Our car is here," Edward told Janet as he put the receiver down.

Chapter 3

The drive to the airport seemed to take far too long to Janet, who was eager to open her envelope and start reading about their assignment.

"We can read on the plane, can't we?" she asked Edward as the driver turned in at airport entrance.

"I'm assuming that we'll be flying first class, which should give us enough privacy to allow for that," Edward replied. "We're being met in the terminal by someone with our tickets and any other documents we might need."

"Documents?" Janet echoed.

"Passports or visas or whatever."

"I have my passport," Janet replied, feeling confused.

Edward chuckled. "You have Janet Markham Bennett's passport. That may not be the passport under which you'll be travelling this weekend, though."

Janet frowned. "I should have realised," she murmured.

"In the past, Mr. Jones has done his best to keep our cover stories as simple as possible, but this assignment might be a bit more complicated," Edward explained as the car pulled to a stop in front of the terminal building.

The driver took their cases out of the car's boot. Edward grabbed one and Janet picked up the other and followed Edward into the building.

"We'll get a luggage cart," Edward said, "and then head towards departures. Someone will recognise us."

A few minutes later, as they wheeled their cart towards the row of ticket windows, a familiar face smiled at Janet from the crowd.

"Christopher," Janet said happily as she pulled the man into a hug.

"Hello," he replied. "I wish we had time for a chat, but you have a plane to catch." He led them to a bench and, once they were all sitting down, opened his briefcase.

"Edward, you're Edward Thomas-Blanchard. You went to boarding school with Arthur's son, John. You've stayed in touch but haven't seen one another in decades. When you noticed on social media that he was planning a trip to the Bahamas, you invited yourself to stay with him on Farntopia."

"I would," Edward said.

Christopher nodded. "At the moment, you're doing everything you can to impress your new wife, Janet Smythson Thomas-Blanchard. She was a wealthy widow when you met her."

"I was?" Janet asked.

Both men chuckled.

"And now Edward, who is worth somewhat less than your first husband, is doing everything he can to spoil you, but you can't help but drop little comments about how your first husband spoiled you even more," Christopher told her. "He was St. John Smythson, by the way."

Janet nodded. "I hope all of this is in the file we were given."

"Actually, it's all in this envelope," Christopher told her, handing her a large envelope. "Your life story and your passport and other important papers. The envelope you got before contains information about the assignment."

Janet nodded and then opened the envelope and pulled out the passport inside. She opened it and then gasped. "I look fabulous," she said as she stared at her photo. "Where did this picture come from? I never look good in passport photos."

Christopher smiled. "Janet Smythson always looks fabulous," he told her.

Janet frowned. "That sounds as if it's going to be hard work."

"Maybe she doesn't try so hard when she's on holiday," Edward suggested.

"Maybe she doesn't try so hard now that St. John is gone," Janet interjected.

Christopher laughed. "Maybe she just naturally looks fabulous. Janet Markham Bennett does, after all."

Janet grinned at him. "You are sweet, but continue. I don't want to miss our flight."

"I'll walk you through. There's no danger of you missing the flight," he assured her. "But I don't really have anything else to tell you. You can read the rest on your journey. You'll have about three hours in the air."

"Someone will meet us at the other end?" Edward asked.

Christopher nodded. "For now, you can give me your passports and anything else you shouldn't be carrying."

Janet went through her handbag and reluctantly handed over her passport, driving license, and credit cards.

"I don't think I have anything else with my name on it," she said as she gave the man her library card.

"Check again," Christopher said, suddenly serious. "I'm not certain what's happening on Farntopia, but I know Mr. Jones is not happy about sending you."

Edward frowned. "Oh?"

"I never said that," Christopher replied. "But I want you both to be very, very careful out there."

"It isn't too late to change your mind," Edward said to Janet.

She shook her head. "Christopher has my credit cards. I'm stuck with Janet Smythson's, um, wow, um, fancy platinum cards." She'd tipped out the contents of the envelope and discovered a stack of credit cards, several of which were branded in ways she'd recently seen in an article about the kinds of cards that the world's richest men and women carried.

"You won't have any use for them on Farntopia," Edward told her.

"I'd better start shopping, then," Janet said as she put Janet Smythson's cards into her purse.

"Let's get you on your plane," Christopher said. He got up and led them to a nearby ticket window. The woman behind it was dealing with another customer, but when Christopher approached, she met his eyes and then nodded and waved anxiously at another woman a few desks away. That woman simply walked away from her customer to greet Janet and Edward. Their tickets and passports were checked, and then their bags were tagged with special labels. Christopher then led them through security, waving some sort of badge at the man who was inspecting tickets. Two minutes later, they reached their departure gate.

"Mr. and Mrs. Thomas-Blanchard, hello," an airline

employee said. "I'm terribly sorry that there isn't time for you to wait in the first-class departure lounge. We'll be boarding in just a few minutes."

Janet smiled thinly. "St. John and I always flew on private jets," she said in a low voice.

Edward frowned. "We talked about that, darling," he said nervously. "We could have done that if it was important to you."

Janet shrugged. "It hardly matters," she said, her tone making it clear that it mattered a great deal.

"I'll leave you here," Christopher said, clearly trying not to laugh. "Have a wonderful time in the Bahamas. Ring me if you need anything."

Janet nodded. "Thank you, darling. We'll ring you when we get back."

He gave her a quick hug. "Take care of yourself," he whispered in her ear. Then he shook Edward's hand. "Take care of Janet," he told him before he turned and walked away.

"Mr. and Mrs. Thomas-Blanchard? We're ready for you to board," they were told a moment later.

Janet felt herself blushing as she and Edward were led past the crowd of people waiting to board the flight. Edward put an arm around her shoulders.

"You do this every day," he reminded her in a whisper.

"Actually, I usually fly in private jets," she shot back with a wink.

He was still laughing when they were shown to their seats. It took him only a moment to shut curtains that went from floor to ceiling around the pair of seats they'd been given.

"That should give us some privacy," Edward said as Janet pulled her two envelopes out of her bag.

"Where should I start?" she asked.

"Start with who you are. You need to memorise that, but it should be fairly simple, I would hope."

Janet read through Janet Smythson's life story. "My goodness, what an interesting life I've led," she told him. "St. John and I had two children, but I haven't spoken to either of them in years. St. John didn't care for them, you see, and I never did anything that might upset St. John."

"Should I care about your children?" Edward asked.

"I suppose either of the ungrateful brats might try getting in touch with you under some sort of pretense or other, but that's a worry for another day. Neither of them will be able to find us in the Bahamas."

Edward nodded. "So they aren't a worry."

"Not unless we allow them to become a worry," Janet told him. "This is my daughter, Ermine." She held up a picture of a bland-looking brunette. "And this is my son, Wolf." She held up another picture and then grinned at Edward as he recognised Christopher Porter's smiling face.

"Interesting," Edward said. "He looks familiar."

"He does, doesn't he?" she replied before she put the pictures to one side and turned her focus to the other envelope.

"Read through everything once, and then we'll have a chat about the family," Edward suggested.

Janet nodded. She sat back in her seat and began to read as the plane taxied down the runway. They were offered food and drinks and duty-free shopping, but they politely declined everything other than water as they both read their way through everything they'd been given.

"We'll be landing in half an hour," Edward said eventually. "Let's talk about what we've read."

"And then we can talk about how much of it we ought to know," Janet suggested. "I can't imagine we're meant to know most of it, really."

Edward nodded. "We'll have that conversation, too," he promised.

Janet turned her pile of papers over and inhaled slowly. "The island is officially named Farnsley Cay, although that wasn't its original name, obviously."

Edward nodded. "But it's been called Farntopia for the last ten years or more by everyone in the family."

"Arthur Farnsley purchased the island thirty-odd years ago, with his second wife, Gloria."

"The second of eleven," Edward added.

Janet giggled. "How does anyone get married eleven times?"

"You'll have to ask Arthur that question."

"I'm not sure he'll be able to answer. The file suggested that he's having great trouble with his memory these days."

Edward nodded. "He's ninety now and has a team of nurses who look after him at his home in London."

"But he's taken only two of them with him to Farntopia," Janet said. "I hope that isn't a mistake."

"He did get approval from his doctors to make the trip, although I suspect it was more a case of him telling them that he was going and them not arguing."

"He's led a colourful life. I'm looking forward to meeting him. I'm sure he has a lot of interesting stories to tell, if he can remember any of them."

"After eleven marriages, he's currently unattached. I believe his son keeps a close eye on that situation."

"I don't blame him, although it seems as if all of his divorces were fairly friendly, and that Arthur managed to keep his fortune largely intact in spite of the number of them."

"All of his money is tied up in complicated trusts," Edward told her. "Did you read the paperwork about the trusts?"

Janet shook her head. "I skimmed it, but it was all legal mumbo jumbo that made less than no sense."

Edward laughed. "That's about right. What it all means is that Arthur is actually penniless, but he's able to live in luxury because the trust pays all of his bills. It's complicated, but it's working for him."

"He's the one who has invited everyone else to the island this weekend."

"And he's there, at least in part, because he's been spending too much time in the UK," Edward told her. "There are tax implications if he's ordinarily resident there."

"I hope the trust and his tax situation aren't relevant to our assignment, because I don't want to have to understand any of that."

"Let's talk about Arthur's only child, John."

"John is sixty. His mother was Arthur's first wife, Genevieve. Sadly, she passed away in a tragic accident not long after John's birth."

"I'd like to know more about that tragic accident," Edward said.

"Oh? Do you think it wasn't an accident?"

"I don't know. The information in the file was incomplete, but it may be that there simply isn't any additional information. I'd like to know what she was doing driving herself through the Alps after midnight during a snowstorm, though."

"Especially with the baby in the car."

Edward nodded. "It was fortunate that he survived the crash. Arthur never had any additional children."

"I can't help but wonder why not. All of his wives were young enough to bear children, and from what I read about them, some of them had children in subsequent relationships as well."

"I'm not certain there's any way to ask Arthur about that without seeming embarrassingly nosy."

"Maybe Janet Smythson is embarrassingly nosy."

"Maybe Janet Smythson should remember that she's Janet Thomas-Blanchard now."

"Janet Smythson Thomas-Blanchard."

Edward chuckled. "Let's get back to the Farnsleys, shall we?"

"In spite of his father's example, or maybe because of it, John has been married only once. His wife, Sarah, is five years younger, and from what I read, spends most of her time and money on treatments to make herself look younger."

Edward found a picture of the woman. "She's had at least two facelifts," he said. "And she's had work done just about everywhere else as well."

Janet frowned. "I'm going to have to work out why Janet Smythson never had any work done."

"Maybe St. John didn't approve."

"He probably didn't, but then he probably cheated as well."

"St. John would never have cheated on you."

"Of course not. We were devoted to one another. Perhaps his sister had a disastrous facelift that frightened me off the idea."

"We'll talk about that later, but we're going to have to give all of these papers to the man who meets our flight. We need to finish going over the family members."

"John and Sarah have three children. Phillip is thirty and married to Rachel who is twenty-eight. Andrew is twenty-eight and married to Stephanie, who is twenty-nine, and Margaret is twenty-six and married to Brandon Rogers, who is forty-one."

Edward nodded. "And none of them have given John and Sarah grandchildren yet."

"Which simplifies things."

Edward laughed. "I suppose it does."

"Phillip and Rachel have been married for four years, which is the longest that any of them have been married. Andrew and Stephanie got married just over a year ago and Margaret and Brandon only got married last month."

"And this is Margaret's second marriage," Edward added. "I hope she isn't planning to beat her grandfather's record."

"Her first husband, Humphrey Davison, was also considerably older. He was thirty-nine when they got married just after her twenty-first birthday. The marriage only lasted for six months, though."

"We're nearly ready to land. Let's talk about the staff who will be on the island while we're there."

"Harold Parker is Arthur's household manager," Janet remembered. "He travels with Arthur everywhere Arthur goes and he's in charge of everything."

"He'll be a very good person to get to know."

Janet nodded. "Stuart Banks is the chef, responsible for preparing all of the meals for the family. I don't envy him the job, having read through the list of special dietary requirements that nearly everyone on the island seems to have."

"It's becoming trendy to need to avoid certain foods, and I think some people are using that as an excuse to tell people they need to avoid anything they don't like, rather than anything to which they're actually allergic."

"I do think that doctors are becoming more aware of how food affects our bodies, though," Janet replied. "And more aware that not everybody can eat the same things all the time. I have a friend who recently discovered at the age of sixty-seven that she's intolerant to gluten. Eliminating it from her diet has changed her life."

Edward nodded. "The last member of staff is Sammy Horton. He's responsible for looking after the house and the entire island. He lives on the island, but the people he manages live elsewhere and travel to the island when they're needed."

"It sounded as if there's a different cleaning woman there every day," Janet said. "And different gardeners and whoever else is needed to keep things running smoothly."

"Which is unfortunate. It seems that Sammy gets his staff from three different agencies, and our agency is going to struggle if they have to investigate every employee at all three of them."

"Perhaps it isn't that complicated. Maybe the same few people come back nearly every day, whatever it says in the file."

"We'll just have to wait and see. That just leaves the nurses."

"Dawn Becker and Audrey Fowler." Janet had to look at the paperwork again to remind herself of their names. "They're both in their mid-thirties and they almost look as if they could be sisters."

"They do have a very similar appearance," Edward said as he studied the pictures of the two women. "There may be any number of reasons for that."

"Maybe Arthur prefers brunettes," Janet suggested.

"Or maybe he prefers blondes, and the family is making sure that he isn't given a chance to meet any blondes," Edward replied.

Janet sighed. "I wish I knew why we are going to Farntopia."

"I do as well," Edward replied. "I hate this assignment

— or rather, I hate this half-assignment. We have no idea what we're going to find when we arrive."

"How often does Smith get involved in things?"

"Smith never gets involved. Smith is above getting involved in assignments. For many years I didn't even know Smith existed. I simply assumed that Mr. Jones, or rather, his predecessor, Mr. Jackson, was running everything."

"But Smith is really in charge?"

"Smith supervises Mr. Jones and a handful of other men and women who do the same sort of job. That may or may not mean that Smith is in charge of the agency."

"I don't understand."

"You aren't meant to understand. No one is meant to understand."

Janet sighed. "Maybe I should have insisted that you stay retired."

"You know we can go home at any time. If our boat isn't handy once we get to Farntopia, then I'll commandeer a helicopter."

Janet stared at him for a moment and then sighed. "St. John would have had a helicopter standing by, just in case," she said.

Edward laughed. "Surely St. John had some faults."

"We'll see," Janet replied as the plane touched down on the runway.

A man in a dark suit and sandals met them in the arrivals hall. He took from them all of the paperwork that they'd been given, locking it into his briefcase. Then he led them outside to a waiting car.

"Enjoy your time sailing in our waters," he told them before he shut the car's door.

"And we're off," Janet said.

"Ready to see our boat?" Edward asked.

"I'm not sure. I'm afraid I might get seasick."

"You can take tablets to help with that," Edward told her. "We're supposed to stay on the boat tonight, but if you're really worried, we can get a room somewhere for tonight and move to the boat tomorrow."

Janet thought for a moment and then shook her head. "Let's stick to the plans that were made for us. I don't want to upset anyone."

"Not yet, anyway," Edward suggested with a grin.

A few minutes later, they reached the docks. The car stopped next to a large luxury yacht. Janet's door was opened, and she was helped out of the car.

"Welcome to your home away from home," the man in the white uniform said brightly. "I'm Captain Donald Jepson, captain of the *Sea Star*."

Janet looked at the yacht and then shrugged. "It's nice enough," she conceded.

Captain Jepson flushed. "It's one of the most luxurious small yachts in the Bahamas. If you'd like to come with me, I'll give you a tour."

Janet looked at Edward, who held out an arm. She took it as two of the ship's crewmembers grabbed their bags and began to walk briskly towards the ship. Janet and Edward followed at a more leisurely pace, lagging behind the captain, who had begun talking about engines and sails and all things boat related.

Chapter 4

Janet did her best to seem bored as the captain took them around a huge sitting room, a spacious dining room, and the huge outdoor deck area. There was a large swimming pool and an additional lap pool for their use, along with a gym and a games room with both electronic games and shelves full of traditional board games and jigsaw puzzles. He introduced them to the other two members of the crew as they went along.

"And this is your cabin," he said eventually, stopping in front of an unmarked door. He reached into his pocket and pulled out a ring of keys. After he unlocked the cabin's door, he handed the key ring to Edward. "Will you need a second key?" he asked.

Edward looked at Janet and shrugged. "I doubt it. We should usually be together."

"If you change your mind, just ask," the captain said before he opened the door and gestured for them to walk inside.

Janet focussed on keeping her breathing even as she surveyed the large and comfortably appointed sitting room.

"You have your own small galley," Captain Jepson told them. "It's been stocked with snacks and drinks. Obviously, our chef will prepare your meals each day."

Edward nodded. "I believe when I booked that you said something about changing the menu options daily."

"Yes, each morning our chef will deliver the day's menu to you. You'll have at least five options for each meal: breakfast, lunch, and dinner. All you'll need to do is circle what you want and then return the menu to the galley," the captain replied.

Janet walked across the room to the sliding doors that led to a huge balcony. She opened the door and stepped outside. As she walked, she could feel the ship bobbing in the water under her feet and, as she grabbed the balcony's railing, she felt a wave of nausea. Frowning, she went back inside and looked at Edward.

"Did you say you had something to help with seasickness?" she asked.

"I do, in my suitcase," Edward replied.

"Every possible remedy has been stocked in the medicine chest in your en-suite," the captain said. He walked across the room and then opened a door. "Through here," he told Janet.

She walked over and stepped into the enormous bedroom. The bed at the centre of the room was round, and she paused for a moment, slightly confused by the idea. Another door opened off the bedroom. Janet crossed to it and found herself in a large bathroom. A huge mirror over the dual sinks covered the medicine chest. Janet opened it and then stared at the fully-stocked shelves.

After a moment's indecision, she grabbed the bottle labelled "fast acting" and quickly read the dosing instructions. After swallowing two tablets, she rejoined Edward and the captain in the sitting room.

The Farnsley Assignment

"We're nearly ready to set sail," Captain Jepson said. "We'll be spending the night at sea, with plans to dock at Farntopia around two o'clock tomorrow."

"Excellent," Edward said.

"Dinner will be served at six," the captain added. "Here's the evening menu. You can simply order when you arrive in the dining room." He handed a sheet of paper to Edward and then turned and walked back to the door. "Don't hesitate to ask if you need anything."

As the door shut behind the man, Janet looked at Edward. "This is gorgeous," she said, her voice squeaking in excitement. "Have you seen the balcony? It's huge, and the views are incredible. Have you seen the bedroom? The bed is round. Why is that even a thing? How do you sleep in a round bed? This room is stunning, too, but the balcony is my favourite thing. I can't believe we have a huge balcony all to ourselves."

"We have the entire yacht all to ourselves," Edward reminded her as he pulled her close. "If you're that fond of the ship, after our weekend with John and Sarah, we should spend a fortnight or more sailing."

"Could we? I mean, maybe – because in addition to being silly excited about how beautiful it all is, I'm also just the tiniest bit seasick."

"Let's see how we do for the next day or so. We don't have to make any decisions yet. For now, we can just relax and enjoy ourselves until we get to Farntopia."

"It's a terrible name," Janet said.

Edward laughed. "It is a terrible name. I can't imagine naming an island after myself."

"Benntopia, Bennhaven, Bennettopia, Bennadise? None of them sound exactly right."

"Farnadise? Would that be better?"

"Farnhaven?"

"Sounds like the horse that won the Grand National in 1967."

Janet laughed. "Maybe that's why Arthur didn't use that. I must say I think I like it better than Farntopia."

Edward opened his mouth to reply, but he stopped when the ship's horn sounded several times before the ship suddenly began to move. Janet gasped and grabbed onto the nearest chair.

"We're moving," she said anxiously.

"Let's go and sit outside," Edward suggested.

Janet followed him onto the balcony and then sank down into the first chair she reached. "We're going awfully quickly."

"Not at all. We're barely moving."

"It feels very fast."

"You need to relax." Edward pulled his chair close to hers and then sat down and pulled her into his arms. "You'll be fine once your body gets used to the movement. Of course, by that time we'll be at Farntopia."

A boat travelling in the opposite direction suddenly appeared. Janet could see two small children playing on the deck. As they sailed past one another, the children both waved at Janet and Edward. She laughed as she waved back.

"I wasn't expecting there to be so much traffic," Janet said sometime later.

"It's a wonderful place to sail."

"Clearly."

"But it's nearly time for our dinner."

Janet sighed. "I'm afraid to eat."

"Are you feeling unwell?"

"Not really, but I'm afraid I might start feeling unwell if I eat something."

"You should eat," Edward told her. "Your tummy will

probably feel better with something in it. You can take a second dose of the seasickness tablets before bed."

The chef prepared them a three-course meal, and Janet couldn't stop herself from eating every bite.

"The soup was delicious, the chicken and vegetables were wonderful, but the chocolate cake was the best part," she told Edward as she pushed her empty pudding plate away from her.

"It was all very good," Edward agreed.

"Of course, St. John and I always ate well when we travelled," Janet added as the chef walked into the room. "He only ever employed men who'd previously owned some of the finest restaurants in the world."

"Was everything to your satisfaction?" the chef asked as he began to clear away their plates.

"Everything was very good," Edward replied.

"It was fine," Janet said. "But I'm quite tired now. Good night." She got to her feet and then turned and left the room, knowing that if she stayed any longer, she'd end up telling the chef how delicious everything had been and struggle to stay in character.

Edward caught up with her as she walked along the upper deck. When he reached her, she'd stopped to admire the view.

"I can't believe we're here," she said softly as she stared at the seemingly endless blue sea.

"It wasn't where we were expecting to be tonight when we got up this morning."

Janet chuckled. "As worrying as this assignment is, part of me loves our complicated, confusing, unexpected life."

"You never rang Joan to tell her that we were leaving New York."

"No, I didn't, did I? I'll have to ring her at some point,

but maybe she won't even notice that we're gone. If we're away for only a weekend, we should be fine."

"And if we decide to sail for longer, you can let her know after the weekend."

"She'd only worry if she knew we were being sent on an assignment, anyway."

Edward chuckled and then pulled her close. "We don't want her to worry," he said softly before he kissed her.

WHEN JANET WOKE up the next morning, she snuggled into Edward's arms and then slowly opened her eyes. For a moment, she was completely disoriented. *Where are we, and why is the bed round?* she wondered before everything came flooding back to her.

"The bed is stupid," she told Edward as they got dressed for the day.

"It isn't that bad."

"Have you ever slept in a round bed before?"

He shrugged. "Once or twice."

"It's a good thing that it's a huge bed, otherwise one or both of us might have ended up on the floor. There aren't any proper edges."

Edward chuckled. "Do you want me to ask Captain Jepson to get us a different bed?"

"I don't want to be any trouble. We'll manage."

"Janet Smythson wouldn't mind being difficult."

"Janet Smythson Thomas-Blanchard has probably slept in round beds before. I'll be fine as long as you snuggle me all night long."

"You know I'm more than happy to oblige."

When Janet left the bedroom, she found the day's menus had been slipped under their door.

"We have to choose breakfast and lunch, but we'll be at Farntopia for dinner," she said to Edward as she handed him his copy of the menu.

"Everything sounds wonderful, but how are you feeling?"

"I think I'm okay. I haven't taken anything for seasickness since bedtime, but I think I'll take something now, just in case. Then I'll be ready for breakfast."

They both selected the full English breakfast and then went and sat on the deck and watched the world go by.

"I'm getting bored," Janet said after the first hour.

"We could swim, play games, or visit the library."

"There's a library?" Janet demanded.

"I was told there is a library. Captain Jepson didn't show us a library on our tour, though."

They asked the first crewmember they saw, and he escorted them to the small library that was tucked in between the much larger gym and the spacious games room. Only one wall was covered in bookshelves, and the shelves were only partially full. It didn't take Janet long to inspect everything that was available.

"If we are going to sail for longer after our visit to Farntopia, remind me to buy a few books," she told Edward as she frowned at the two titles that were all that she was interested in reading from the options in the ship's library.

"If we do decide to sail for a while, we'll plan lots of shore excursions," he told her. "That doesn't mean you can't buy several books as well, but it does mean we won't be stuck on the ship for hours on end."

Edward grabbed a book, seemingly at random, and then followed Janet back up on to the main deck. They settled in and read until it was time for lunch.

"I'm not cut out for a life of leisure," Janet said as she

and Edward walked towards the dining room. "I enjoyed this morning, but I wouldn't want to do this every day."

Edward grinned at her. "But this is exactly the way that Janet Smythson lives," he reminded her.

Janet sighed. "I'm going to forget when it really matters and mess up everything."

"You'll be fine," Edward assured her. "Just try to be less nice."

Be less nice, Janet reminded herself a few hours later, as she and Edward prepared to disembark at Farntopia. She checked for the tenth time that she'd packed everything and then looked at Edward.

"I'm as ready as I'll ever be," she said nervously.

"No matter what, remember that I love you," Edward said before he grabbed their suitcases and headed for the door.

"Good afternoon," the man standing on the dock said as Janet and Edward made their way off the ship. To Janet, he looked like Hollywood's idea of the perfect butler. She knew he was in his early fifties. His grey hair was cut short, and he was wearing a black suit in spite of the hot weather.

"Good afternoon," Janet replied.

"Hello," Edward said. "I'm Edward Thomas-Blanchard and this is my wife, Janet."

"Janet Smythson Thomas-Blanchard," Janet said.

The man smiled. "I'm Harold Parker. I'm Mr. Arthur Farnsley's executive assistant."

"I haven't seen John's father in decades," Edward said. "I do hope he doesn't mind that I invited myself to stay for the weekend."

Harold hesitated before he replied. "You're more than welcome," he said flatly.

Or maybe not, Janet thought.

"Ah, Sammy, there you are," Harold said as another man joined them.

Janet knew that the new arrival was around the same age as Harold, but she thought he looked younger. His hair was pulled back into a long ponytail, and he was wearing dirty jeans and a torn T-shirt. He grinned at Harold. "Am I late?"

"No more than usual," Harold replied coolly.

Sammy grinned at Janet. "It's hard to get good help down here," he said with a wink.

Janet forced herself not to smile as she tried to work out how Janet Smythson would react to the man's attitude.

"This is Sammy Horton," Harold said, saving Janet from having to reply. "He takes care of maintenance and the day-to-day running of the island."

"I take care of everything," Sammy interjected. "And for the next twenty-four hours or so, there's only going to be me to do it. We're supposed to get a storm, so no one else will be coming out tonight."

Janet frowned. "A storm?"

"Just some wind and rain. We're a few weeks away from hurricane season," Harold assured her. "It's nothing that should worry you."

"What about power?" Edward asked.

"We have solar power, and we also have backup generators that can power the entire island if they have to," Harold replied. "The only thing we'll be missing is a few of the maids that help with the cleaning and the cooking."

"Which means I'll get roped into helping in the kitchen tonight," Sammy said. "Stuart will make me peel potatoes and chop vegetables, even if you aren't having either of those things for your dinner."

"If you'd care to follow me," Harold said tightly, "I'll show you to your cottage."

"Cottage?" Janet echoed, looking at Edward. "You didn't mention that we would be staying in a cottage."

"I'm certain it will be lovely," Edward told her.

Janet frowned and then folded her arms. "A cottage?"

"You'll want to send your captain on his way," Harold said. "He'll want to get the ship in a safe harbour before the storm begins."

Edward nodded. He turned and waved at Captain Jepson, who was standing on the deck watching them. After Edward waved, the captain gave them a small bow and then turned and walked away. Janet frowned as the crew untied the ship from the dock and then jumped on board.

"What if we aren't happy here?" she demanded.

"We can endure anything for one night," Edward told her. "I can ring Captain Jepson at any time and get him back."

"I don't know about this cottage," Janet said.

"If you'd care to follow me," Harold suggested.

Janet sighed deeply and then fell into step behind the man, who'd turned and begun to walk along the well-worn path that led inland. Sammy picked up their suitcases and followed.

"The cottages were all completed in the last ten years," Harold said as they walked. "Mr. Farnsley had one built for each of the grandchildren when they reached eighteen. He felt that each of them should have his or her own private space at that age. While he was building those three cottages, he added an additional half-dozen for guests."

"How crowded," Janet murmured.

"But no one is staying here at the moment, aside from Mr. Farnsley, his son, his grandchildren, and all of the spouses," Harold told her.

"Oh, dear," Edward said. "It does sound as if I chose the wrong weekend to impose."

"Mr. Farnsley has quite fond memories of you from when you and John were at school together," Harold told him. "When John told Mr. Farnsley that you were having a sailing holiday, Mr. Farnsley was more than happy to agree to your joining the party here."

"Well, that's good to hear. I have fond memories of Mr. Farnsley as well. I didn't really expect him to remember me, though," Edward said.

"I'll warn you that Mr. Farnsley's memory isn't as good as it had been formerly," Harold told him. "If he doesn't recognise you or remember you when you meet him, please don't be disappointed."

"Not at all," Edward replied. "My own father doesn't remember me any longer. We all get older."

Harold paused as the path branched off in two different directions.

"If you follow that path, it will lead you to the main house," he told Janet and Edward. "Dinner will be served there at seven tonight. Both Mr. Farnsley and his son, John, are staying in the main house, along with John's wife, Sarah. Your cottage is down this way."

He turned down the other path and, after a moment, Janet realised that they were heading back towards the water. A short while later, they walked around a bend. Janet nearly gasped at the stunning white sandy beach in front of her. It was only after they'd walked a bit farther that she noticed the row of cottages. They were set back from the water, and strategically planted trees and shrubs helped them disappear into the landscape. Each was two storeys high, with huge balconies jutting out from the upper storeys.

Janet gave Edward's hand an excited squeeze as they continued down the beach.

"Mr. Phillip Farnsley and his wife, Rachel, are staying in this cottage," Harold told them, gesturing towards the first cottage in the row. "The second cottage is currently being occupied by Mr. Andrew Farnsley and his wife, Stephanie. The third cottage is where you will be staying."

"And are any of the other cottages occupied?" Edward asked as they walked down the short path that led to the third cottage's door.

"The next cottage along, number four, is occupied," Harold replied. "Mr. Brandon Rogers and his wife, Margaret, nèe Farnsley, are staying there." He stopped at the front door to their cottage and reached into a pocket. "Here are your keys. Enjoy your stay."

He dropped the keys into Edward's hand and then turned and walked away.

Janet frowned. "That's it?" she demanded.

Edward grinned at her. "I'm sure we can find everything inside."

"I'm happy to give you the grand tour," Sammy offered as he opened the door to the cottage from the inside. "I've left your cases in the main bedroom."

"Thank you," Edward said. "I don't believe we need a tour."

"Mrs. Thomas-Blanchard, is there anything I can do for you?" Sammy asked.

Janet gave him a small smile. "No, but thank you," she replied.

He shrugged. "I'll see you in the main house around seven, then. They'll start having cocktails around six, just so you know."

He was gone, disappearing down the path before Janet or Edward could reply.

"Shall we?" Edward asked, offering his arm.

They walked into the cottage together. Janet waited until he'd shut the door before she spoke.

"This is so beautiful," she said as she walked into the middle of the comfortable sitting room. "I love everything about it. The colours are beachy and cosy at the same time, and look at the views."

Edward nodded. "There's nothing that compares to looking out on the water."

Janet took a quick walk through the kitchen, bedroom, and bathroom on the lower level before rushing up the stairs. There, she stuck her head into another bedroom with its own en-suite before walking into the enormous main bedroom. She barely noticed the huge bed and didn't bother investigating the en-suite. Instead, she flung open the double doors that led to the balcony and walked outside.

"I want to stay here forever," she told Edward when he joined her.

"It is spectacular," he agreed as they stood together watching the waves washing up on the beach below them.

"And the cottages are staggered just enough to make the balcony feel private, even though it isn't," Janet said.

"…dies we'll be able to do whatever we want." The words floated across the beach.

"Here's hoping he dies soon, then," was the unpleasant reply.

Chapter 5

Janet and Edward both stood silently for several minutes, waiting to hear more, but they could hear nothing but the sound of the waves and the shouts of the seagulls above them.

"Who was that?" Janet asked. "And who are they hoping dies soon?"

"It must have been one of the grandchildren with a spouse," Edward said. "I can't imagine that sound travels well enough for us to have heard Phillip and Rachel talking, so it must have been Andrew and his wife or Margaret and her husband. The first voice sounded masculine and the second feminine."

Janet nodded. "Now I'm worried that someone wants to kill poor Arthur Farnsley."

"Perhaps they were talking about John's death," Edward suggested.

"I suppose it all depends on what is in each of the men's wills."

"I believe all of Arthur's money is tied up in trusts. I'm not certain what will happen when he dies."

"What about John's money?"

"I'm not certain that John has any money of his own. I believe he may simply live off the income from his own trust. Each of the grandchildren has a personal trust fund as well. I don't believe any of them has ever held down a job."

"I can't imagine not working. I'll admit that there were times when I found teaching difficult and frustrating, but I also really loved my job. Running the bed and breakfast is a different matter, of course."

"You don't love the bed and breakfast?"

"I love Doveby House, but I don't love having guests. Some of our guests have been wonderful, and I haven't hated having them in the house, but if it were up to me, we'd stop having guests and simply enjoy Doveby House ourselves."

"But Joan loves having guests."

Janet nodded. "And we haven't been back to Doveby Dale in over a month, so I can't complain, can I? Joan is in Derbyshire, trying to keep impossibly difficult people happy, while I'm here on a private beach in the Caribbean. I win."

Edward chuckled. "I don't think Joan would be at all tempted to trade lives with you."

"No, she'd hate the assignment that's brought us here. Adventure isn't a word that anyone would ever associate with Joan."

"And yet, she started her own business after she'd retired. That's an adventure of a sort."

"Are you suggesting we should invite Joan to join us on our next assignment?"

Edward laughed. "Not even the tiniest bit," he said as he pulled her close.

Some minutes later, Janet glanced at her watch. "We

need to get ready for dinner," she said. "Do you want to be at the main house in time for cocktails?"

"I think we should arrive around half six. I can't help but feel as if we're crashing the party here, but we must act completely oblivious, or we'll end up getting ourselves uninvited."

"Are you concerned about what we heard earlier?" Janet asked as she dug through her suitcase.

"At this point, I'm concerned about everything," was Edward's worrying reply.

"Harold said that Mr. Farnsley remembers you," Janet said once she was ready to go. "How is that even possible?"

"No doubt John introduced his father to dozens of his school friends when he was younger. Arthur has probably confused me with someone who has a similar name."

"Or maybe he knows who you are really are and why you're here," Janet mused. "Someone on the island is friends with Smith. It could be Arthur."

"Or John or one of the grandchildren or one of the spouses or one of the staff."

Janet frowned. "Have you ever met any of Smith's friends before?"

Edward chuckled. "Not to my knowledge, but I may have. I'm unaware of ever having met Smith, as well, but I may have."

"This spy business is more complicated than I realised."

"I probably should explain a bit better," Edward admitted. "Smith isn't so much a person as a position. He or she is head of the agency, or maybe simply head of part of the agency. I've never questioned the chain of command. I've had four different handlers over the decades, and they've all reported to Smith. Mr. Jones is the most recent to have that position."

"He or she?"

Edward shrugged. "I know nothing about Smith. I'm not even informed when the person holding Smith's position changes. I have to assume that the Smith that sent us here isn't the same Smith who was working for the agency when I was hired forty-odd years ago."

"But they've all been called Smith?"

"They've all been called Smith."

"He or she could be anyone."

"Indeed. He or she could even be someone I know. I've worked with a number of different agents over the years. Any one of them might have decided to get out of the field."

"But this is the first time that Smith has asked you for a favour."

"It is, and that's part of what makes this assignment so frustrating. I feel as if Smith is worried about someone, but because we haven't been given any information, we've no idea whom we need to protect."

"It must be Arthur or John," Janet speculated.

Edward looked at his watch. "We should go."

Janet nodded and then picked up her handbag. She checked that her very expensive-looking earrings were in place and then looked at the bracelet on her arm. "The jewellery that the agency provided is stunning."

"We can keep it."

Janet laughed. "I can't imagine I'll ever have an occasion to wear any of it again. Janet Markham Bennett doesn't go anywhere fancy."

"She could," Edward offered as they walked out of their cottage. "But now we must find our way to the main house," he said as he shut the door behind them.

"All of this sand is going to ruin my shoes," Janet complained.

"You can buy new shoes."

"I will, and you'll be paying for them," she snapped.

Edward sighed. "Darling, I'm sorry about the sand. It never occurred to me that we'd have to walk anywhere."

Janet shrugged. "I don't have to tell you that this isn't my idea of a holiday."

"No, darling, I quite understand."

The walk to the house took only a few minutes. Edward knocked, and a moment later Harold opened the door to let them in.

Janet was happy to step into the air-conditioned interior of the huge home.

"It's very hot out there," she said.

Harold nodded. "I'm terribly sorry about that, but please come through to the drawing room. I know John is looking forward to seeing you."

Janet put a reluctant smile on her face as she and Edward followed Harold down a short corridor. While she knew the agency had prepared things for their stay, she was suddenly terrified that John was going to take one look at Edward and deny having ever met him before. The drawing room felt crowded to Janet as they entered.

"Ah, there he is," a voice said. "Thomas-Bank Card, how the devil are you?"

Edward chuckled and then shook hands with the man who had to be John Farnsley. He had grey hair and he was wearing expensive-looking leisurewear. "Farce-Ley, it's good to see you again," Edward said.

"You must remember Sarah," John said, stepping back and then sliding an arm around his wife.

Sarah smiled, and Janet thought she looked nervous. That may just have been because her face barely moved, though. It was unnaturally smooth and expertly made up. She was wearing an evening gown that wouldn't have looked out of place on a Hollywood red carpet and what appeared to be a fortune in diamond jewellery. "It's nice to see you again," Sarah said.

"She's still cross with me because I drove into your swimming pool," Edward said with a laugh.

Sarah's eyes went slightly wider and then she shrugged. "Of course, it was an accident."

Edward and John both laughed heartily.

"Of course it was," John agreed, still chuckling.

"But meet my lovely wife, Janet Smythson Thomas-Blanchard," Edward said, reaching out and pulling Janet closer. "Janet, this is John Farnsley and his better half, Sarah."

"It's very nice to meet you both," Janet replied.

Sarah nodded. "Those are lovely earrings."

Janet put a hand to one ear. "My darling St. John bought them for me on a business trip somewhere. He always brought me fabulous gifts when he travelled, and he travelled a great deal. After all the years we were together, I'm afraid I've forgotten exactly where he found these."

"I can't see that it matters," Edward muttered.

"But come and meet the family," John said. "The last time I saw you, the children were babies. I've no doubt none of them remember you."

"I can't believe I don't remember someone driving into the swimming pool," the man standing next to John said.

"That particular incident happened when we were on holiday before you were even born," John told him. "Your mother and I hadn't been married for long, and the holiday home belonged to a dear friend of hers. We'd all been behaving impeccably up to that point."

"I wouldn't have said that," Sarah said.

John laughed again. "But this is Phillip, my oldest," he told Edward as he gestured towards the man next to him.

Janet studied the man, who had dark hair and eyes. He was taller than his father and better dressed. He shook hands with Edward and then briefly touched Janet's hand before waving in the direction of the bar that was set up along the back wall of the room.

"My other half, Rachel, is at the bar," he said. "Rachel, wave!" he shouted.

The beautiful brunette who had been chatting with the man behind the bar turned and then gave them all a small wave. She was wearing a pretty sundress that showed off her slender figure. When she waved, Janet noticed the row of diamond and gemstone bracelets that almost seemed to cover the woman's arm.

"Now you've done it," John said. "Edward has seen the bar, and now the drinking will commence."

Edward laughed and then shook his head. "I'm a reformed man – well, semi-reformed, anyway. I don't drink nearly as much as I did formerly. But if you insist, then I will have a drink now. Darling, what can I get for you?"

"Dry white wine," Janet replied.

John led them over to the bar. "Stuart, take excellent care of my friends," he said. "While he gets your drinks, I'll round up the other children."

Edward ordered drinks as John walked over to the couple who were standing together near the windows. He said something to them that made the man frown, but a moment later they followed John back to the bar.

"My second son, Andrew, and his lovely wife, Stephanie," John performed the introduction.

Andrew had light brown hair and glasses and didn't really look much like his father or his brother. Stephanie was blonde, with long hair pulled back into a low knot at the back of her neck. They were both wearing shorts and

T-shirts. His advertised a well-known brand of beer, and hers bore the name of a large US university.

"It's nice to meet you," Andrew said. "How are you finding the island?"

"It's fine," Janet replied as she reached for her glass of wine.

"Fine?" Andrew echoed.

Janet shrugged. "I've never stayed anywhere without staff before, aside from hotels, although we often hired at least one or two people to look after us when we stayed in hotels over the years."

"Sammy can arrange for someone from the next island to come over and look after you while you're here," John said. "He can have someone here in the morning."

"We'll see. Edward assures me that we can survive on our own for the weekend."

"I'm looking forward to having a bit of privacy, actually," Edward said. "We're staying on a small yacht and sailing around the islands at the moment, and everywhere we go on the ship, we seem to trip over a member of the crew."

"Which is how is should be," Janet argued. "That way our needs can be met quickly."

"If you need anything while you're here, you simply have to ring the main house. Harold and Sammy will be able to help you," John assured them.

Janet did her best to look unconvinced and slightly annoyed, but she wasn't certain she'd managed it.

"And last but not least, my daughter, Margaret, and her husband, Brandon Rogers," John said after an awkward silence. He gestured towards the couple who were standing nearby, clearly listening to the conversation.

Brandon was obviously some years older than his wife. His dark hair was liberally sprinkled with grey. He was wearing a pair of black trousers and a grey button-down shirt with a tie. Margaret was a pretty brunette who looked more like Phillip and her father than Andrew or her mother. She was wearing a short white robe and hadn't bothered to tie it around herself, which meant Janet got a good look at the tiny pink bikini she was wearing under the robe.

"Hi," Margaret said brightly. "It's always fun to have visitors on the island. You'll have to tell me stories about Daddy's school days."

Edward nodded. "I'd be more than happy to tell you stories about your father's school days," he said with a wink.

"That won't be necessary," John interjected. "I've told my children every interesting story from my past."

"Why don't I believe that?" Edward asked with a chuckle.

"I'm certain Daddy can't have been as boring as he wants us to believe," Margaret said.

"He's told you he was boring?" Edward asked. "We really do need to talk."

Margaret laughed. "How wonderful. We should have lunch together tomorrow."

"We were going to take a picnic to the waterfall tomorrow," Brandon objected.

Margaret looked at him for a moment and then shrugged. "We can do that anytime."

"But we're only here for the weekend," he protested.

Margaret sighed and then patted his arm. "We'll work it out," she said.

Brandon looked as if he wanted to argue, but after a moment, he shrugged. "Of course, darling," he said.

The grandfather clock in the corner of the room began to chime. A moment later, the room's door swung open.

"Father," John said, rushing forwards to offer the man in the doorway his arm.

The pair took a few a steps into the room and then stopped. The young woman who'd walked in behind Arthur quickly pulled a chair into place behind him. John helped him lower himself into the chair and then stepped back.

"How are you tonight?" he asked Arthur.

"Tired," the man replied. "Always tired."

John nodded. "We could have dinner earlier tomorrow," he suggested.

"We always have dinner at seven," Arthur replied. "But who are all of these people?"

John took a deep breath before he replied. "You remember Sarah," he began, nodding at his wife.

"If that's Sarah, she's had a new face since the last time I saw her," Arthur snapped.

Rachel and Stephanie both started to laugh. Phillip gave his wife an angry look while Andrew grinned at Stephanie.

"She spends a fortune on creams and lotions and potions," John told his father.

"Her fortune, I hope," he replied.

John nodded. "Of course," he said in a low voice.

"Phillip? Andrew?" Arthur barked.

The two men both jumped and then walked closer to their grandfather.

"We're here," Andrew said.

Arthur looked them up and down and then sighed. "With your wives?"

"Yes, of course," Phillip said.

The two women rushed to join their husbands.

Arthur looked at them all for a moment and then

looked past them. "And Margaret, my only granddaughter. What happened to Humphrey?"

"I traded him for a better model," Margaret replied. "You were at my wedding when I married Brandon," she added, gesturing towards her husband.

Arthur frowned. "Can't say as I mind not remembering that," he muttered before he looked over at Edward and Janet.

"Who are they?" he demanded.

"You remember Edward Thomas-Blanchard," John said. "We went to school together, and, when I told you that they were sailing in the area, you invited them to join us for the weekend."

"I did? What was I thinking? I've several things to discuss with all of you, and the last thing I want is strangers in the house," Arthur replied.

"We don't mean to impose," Edward said quickly. "Janet and I can leave in the morning, if you'd prefer."

"But, Father, you did invite them," John added.

"Janet?" Arthur asked.

"Janet Smythson Thomas-Blanchard," Janet said, walking over and offering her hand. "It's a great pleasure to meet you. You may have known my first husband, St. John Smythson."

Arthur took her hand and squeezed it tightly. "St. John was a true gentleman," he said. "We did a few deals together over the decades, although not as many as I would have liked, actually. I always made money when I went in with St. John. He had a Midas touch, that man."

Janet nodded. "He passed away nearly ten years ago, but I still miss him."

"And now you're married to Thomas Bank Card? Oh, I remember his childhood nickname only too well. The poor boy struggled to make friends, but was able to buy quite a few, weren't you?" he asked Edward.

Edward shrugged. "My parents gave me a generous allowance."

"And you shared that allowance with anyone and everyone," Arthur said.

Before Edward could reply, Harold walked into the room. He walked to the back wall and then used a large mallet to strike the gong hanging there. "Dinner is served," he announced before he walked back out of the room.

"Good," Arthur said. "We have a great deal to discuss over dinner. Edward, Janet, you may as well stay. Perhaps it will be helpful to have witnesses this evening."

He struggled to his feet and then, leaning heavily on his son's arm, made his way out of the room. Sarah followed. The grandchildren seemed to fall into place behind her, with Phillip and Rachel going first, followed by Andrew and Stephanie. Brandon and Margaret brought up the rear, leaving Janet and Edward to follow them.

Chapter 6

The dining room had wood-panelled walls and a huge crystal chandelier over a long rectangular table that could easily have seated twenty people. Arthur took his seat at the table's head and then watched as the others all took their seats.

Janet and Edward stood back and waited as John sat next to his father on the right, with Sarah on his other side. Phillip sat on Arthur's left side and Rachel slid into the other seat next to him. Andrew took the empty seat next to his mother, with his wife on his other side. Margaret told Brandon to sit next to Rachel, and then she sat down on his other side.

"You go and sit next to Stephanie," Edward suggested to Janet. "I'll sit next to Margaret. That will keep the table balanced."

Janet frowned and then shrugged. "Whatever," she said airily before she walked over and sat down.

Once Edward was seated, Harold began to fill wine glasses.

"Where is Heidi?" Arthur demanded.

"Sammy has sent everyone home," Harold told him. "We're supposed to get some bad weather later, so he let everyone leave early."

"How bad?" John asked.

"Just wind and rain. It's too early in the year for hurricanes," Harold assured him.

Stuart and Harold served the soup course a few moments later. As they left the room, Arthur cleared his throat.

"I'm not going to be around for much longer," he said.

"You mustn't say such things," Sarah protested.

Arthur shrugged. "It's true. I'm ninety, and I'm starting to forget things. I'd rather go sooner than later if later means losing my quality of life. I'm forgetting more and more every day. I've already forgotten what you looked like when you married John."

Rachel used her napkin to hide her face while Stephanie tried to turn her laughter into a cough.

"You still have a few good years left," John said heartily.

"Maybe, but maybe not. I've been talking to my solicitors. We've been reworking some of the trusts," Arthur told them.

"I thought they couldn't be touched," John said, sounding concerned.

"Good solicitors can always find ways," Arthur told him. "They have to be very good, though. At least seven of my wives had good solicitors who tried hard to get their hands on my money. They all failed, of course."

"What have you done to the trusts, then?" Phillip asked.

"I've moved some of the money from each of them into a new trust," he explained.

"How much money?" John asked.

"Different amounts from each trust," Arthur said. "I've cut yours in half, because you've already enjoyed living off of my money for sixty years."

"In half?" Sarah gasped. "But we can't survive on half of our usual income."

"I'm certain you'll find a way," Arthur said, sounding unconcerned. "Maybe one or both of you could find a job."

Sarah put her hand to her chest and simply stared at her father-in-law.

"Father, you can't mean that," John said.

"What about the rest of us?" Phillip asked.

"I've taken a quarter out of each of your trusts," Arthur told him.

"That isn't so bad," John replied, sounding relieved.

"You should be fine," Arthur told him. "Andrew, on the other hand, may have a problem."

"What problem?" Andrew asked.

"I want you to agree to a DNA test," Arthur told him. "You look nothing like my son and a great deal like the man that Sarah was involved with before she and my son were married."

"What are you suggesting?" Sarah asked.

Janet assumed she was shocked, even though the emotion didn't appear on the woman's nearly frozen face.

"I'm suggesting that you had an affair," Arthur replied. "If you didn't, then you've no reason to object to a DNA test for Andrew."

"I object on principle," Sarah replied. "I object because I'm hurt and shocked and angry that you could even suggest such a thing."

"Sir, we're ready for the main course," Harold said from the room's doorway.

Arthur smiled and sat back in his seat. "You may

serve," he said before he sat back and watched as Harold and Sammy cleared away the soup bowls and served the main course. As the door shut behind the two men, Sarah inhaled slowly.

"I can't believe that you're accusing me of cheating," she said angrily. "Especially considering how many times John has cheated on me."

"I've never cheated," John protested.

Sarah looked at him and then laughed. "Your father may believe you, but I don't. What about Julie Dixon?"

John frowned. "Julie managed some of my accounts for a few years. We had a good working relationship."

"And you took her to the Algarve for a holiday," Sarah said.

"I went to the Algarve, and she happened to be there at the same time," John countered.

"And you stayed together in the same hotel room," Sarah said.

"We shared a large suite with two bedrooms," John told her.

Sarah sighed. "And you shared just one of those bedrooms. Please, can you stop lying to me? I have photos and evidence."

"Have you been saving them up so you can fight for a big divorce settlement?" Margaret asked.

"Divorce?" Sarah echoed. "I'm not planning on getting a divorce. Your father has his faults, but we've been together for over thirty years. I can't imagine anything that would make me leave him."

"And you wouldn't get much if you did divorce John," Arthur said. "All of my former wives will attest to that. But we were discussing Andrew's parentage. Here is what I'm willing to offer. If you don't want Andrew to take a DNA test, then he can keep a quarter of his current trust as long as you admit that you had an affair and that you aren't certain who fathered Andrew."

Sarah stared at him. "I'm not admitting to anything," she said angrily.

"In that case, Andrew, if you want to keep your trust, you'll have to take a DNA test," Arthur told him.

"I'm not sure I'm prepared to do that," Andrew said.

"If you refuse, your trust will be dissolved and everything in it will go into the new trust that I'm creating," Arthur told him.

"What if I take the test and it proves that I'm not your grandson?" Andrew asked.

"Then you lose your trust," Arthur replied.

Andrew looked at Sarah. "What are the odds that your husband isn't my father?" he demanded.

Sarah frowned at him. "I didn't have an affair," she said unconvincingly.

"I don't suppose your lover would welcome a new son into his family," Andrew said bitterly.

"If your biological father was who I think it was, he died in a car crash over a decade ago," Arthur told him. "In the years before his death, he'd managed to burn through his family's entire fortune. There were some who believed that he'd crashed on purpose because he knew he was so far in debt that he'd never recover."

Sarah shook her head. "Timothy would never have crashed on purpose. He loved life too much."

"Regardless, Andrew, you have some decisions to make," Arthur said. "And so do you," he told Margaret.

She frowned. "I look just like Daddy," she said quickly.

Arthur laughed. "I'm not worried about your parentage, but I am worried about your future."

"My future? We'll survive on a quarter less income. We'll be fine."

"I don't want you to end up as I did, with eleven failed marriages behind you."

"I won't," Margaret said carelessly. "Brandon and I are going to be together forever."

"I hope you mean that," Arthur told her. "Your income depends on it."

"What does that mean?" Margaret demanded.

Arthur smiled at her. "You have six months to make any changes to your life that you'd care to make. After that six months, if you get another divorce, you'll lose your trust."

Margaret stared at him.

Brandon frowned. "You're encouraging her to divorce me in the next six months," he said.

Arthur shrugged. "Only if she isn't one hundred per cent certain that your marriage is going to last forever," he replied.

"But how can I possibly be certain?" Margaret asked. "What if, thirty years from now, Brandon decides to leave me? That won't be my fault."

"Do you think you've married a man who would do such a thing?" Arthur asked.

Margaret frowned. "I've no idea. I mean, it never really mattered before. If things got bad, either of us could leave. But now we can't. We're both stuck forever."

"Unless you divorce him in the next six months," Rachel reminded her.

Margaret looked at Brandon, and it was clear to Janet that she was giving that idea some serious thought.

"But what about the new trust?" John asked. "What is that all about?"

"Ah, yes, the new trust," Arthur said. "That goes to my first great-grandchild."

Janet froze in her seat as the room went completely

silent. She met Edward's eyes and he raised an eyebrow. *No one was expecting that, then,* Janet thought as she very carefully put her fork down.

"You want one of us to give you a great-grandchild," Phillip said.

"Not especially, but the more I thought about it, the more I realised that I don't trust any of you to properly look after the next generation. Oh, the trusts will all continue, but my fortune has already been divided between my son and three grandchildren. As each of you have children, the trusts will be divided further and further until each one is barely worth having. I decided that my first great-grandchild deserved something more," Arthur explained.

"So now we have to race each other to get pregnant," Margaret said unhappily. "And I have to try to get pregnant in the middle of a divorce."

"What happens if I fail my DNA test?" Andrew asked.

"Then your child won't be my great-grandchild," Arthur replied.

"All of this is just your way of favouring Phillip yet again," Andrew complained. "He's always been your favourite grandchild, and now he's the one who will benefit the most from what you're doing."

Arthur shrugged. "You may believe that if it makes you feel better about things. When you reach ninety and look back on your own life, maybe you'll be able to begin to understand my behaviour. I'm doing what I believe is best for the family as a whole, even if certain individuals may be hurt by my actions."

"So, Daddy has lost half of his income. Andrew may lose everything if he fails a DNA test, even though his parentage isn't in any way his fault. And I've lost a quarter of my income and have only six months to make a final decision on my marriage and, hopefully, get pregnant. Meanwhile, Phillip has lost a quarter of his income, but if he can have a baby quickly enough, he'll get control over the baby's huge trust fund," Margaret said bitterly.

"And if Rachel can't or won't get pregnant, he can divorce her and try again with someone else," Andrew added. "You're the only one being trapped in your marriage."

"Or out of it and doomed to remain single forever," Margaret said.

"This is crazy," John said. "You can't be serious."

"Is everyone ready for pudding?" Arthur asked.

"I'm quite finished," Margaret said, putting her napkin on the table and getting up from her chair.

Brandon quickly shoved a large bite of chicken into his mouth and then jumped up.

"Sit," Arthur told them. "Stuart made me a birthday cake."

Margaret looked as if she wanted to argue.

"Sit," her father said flatly.

Dropping back into her chair, Margaret sighed dramatically. "This isn't a family gathering, it's a hostage situation," she muttered.

The words were barely out of her mouth when the lights suddenly went out. Janet resisted the urge to scream, not that anyone would have noticed as several other women began to shriek. After a moment, the lights flickered back on.

"We've lost power," Harold said as he rushed into the room. "We're running off of the generators now. We should be able to keep them running all night, but we need to be careful with our electricity usage."

"Ring for the ship," Janet said to Edward.

He shook his head. "If the weather is bad enough to

have knocked out the power here, then we don't want to be out on the water in it."

Janet frowned as everyone else began to speak at once. After a minute of angry confusion, Arthur held up a hand.

"Enough," he said firmly. "We'll have to have our cake tomorrow," he said when everyone stopped talking and looked at him. "For now, let's move back into the drawing room. We can have a drink or two and keep an eye on the weather. If it doesn't improve, Harold and Sammy will have to take you all home in one of the golf carts."

The corridor was only dimly lit. Janet held Edward's hand as they followed the others back into the drawing room. The curtains that had covered the windows had been pulled back, revealing dark skies. A bright flash of lightning made Janet jump.

Harold moved behind the bar and quickly began pouring drinks. A few minutes later, everyone was gathered on couches and chairs arranged in a rough circle. Arthur had taken a seat with his back to the windows, but the others all tried to position themselves so that they could see what was happening outside while they drank.

"I need to speak on behalf of my children," John said after a long and awkward silence. "I'm not going to complain about you cutting my income in half, although I could. I do think that what you're doing to my children is unfair, though."

"Are you including Andrew in that?" Arthur asked with a nasty grin.

John hesitated and then nodded. "Andrew has been raised as my son and I consider him my son, regardless of his DNA. As Margaret said, his parentage isn't his fault, and if Sarah did have an affair, I've accepted Andrew as my child and never felt the need to test his DNA. It's unnecessary and unfair to question his parentage now."

"And you can't understand why I would prefer to leave my money to my own flesh and blood, rather than to the offspring of a stranger?" Arthur asked.

"This is Andrew you're talking about," Sarah said. "You held him for the first time when he was two days old. You watched him learn to walk and taught him his first naughty word when he was three. You bought him his first car before he'd earned his license, and you sent him on a gap year trip around the world before he went to uni. You've always loved and treated him as your grandchild."

"When you put it that way, he's done pretty well for himself, considering we aren't related," Arthur said.

Andrew sighed. "I'm tempted to get the DNA test, just so I can see your face when you find out that you're wrong."

"I'm not wrong," Arthur replied.

"He's twenty-eight," Sarah said. "Surely, if you're going to be this cruel, you should have done it years ago."

"I didn't know years ago," Arthur replied. "Years ago, I simply assumed that Andrew more closely resembled your side of the family. I never thought to question who his father might have been. I never imagined that you'd cheated on John."

"What's changed?" Edward asked.

"That hardly matters," Arthur replied.

"Someone with malicious intent must have said something," John said. "He or she must be trying to destroy our family."

"No one is destroying anything," Arthur replied with a wave of his hand. "I was provided with certain information, that's all."

"Information that you chose to believe, no matter what we say," Sarah said.

"It will be simple enough for you to prove that information wrong," he countered. "DNA tests are easy enough to obtain these days."

"Exactly what information were you given?" John demanded.

Arthur frowned. "I wasn't going go into the details, but I've been furnished with evidence that Sarah was involved with another man around the time that Andrew was most likely conceived, based on his date of birth."

"He's my son," John said firmly. "Whatever a DNA test shows, he's my son."

"Thank you," Andrew said.

John nodded at him. "If you choose to cut him off, I'll find a way to provide for him."

Arthur laughed. "With your reduced income, you'll struggle to support yourself and Sarah."

"We'll find a way," John told him. "I think I've had enough of this."

"What else were you told?" Sarah asked. "What's behind the threats to Margaret?"

"They aren't threats," Arthur replied. "I'm simply doing what I can to try to improve her life." He looked over at Margaret and smiled. "You know I've always adored you, my only granddaughter. I didn't care for Humphrey, and I don't care for Brandon, either. I think you should be more careful in choosing husbands, and also in how you spend your spare time."

"What does that mean?" Margaret asked.

"You spend a great deal of time with a young man named Dominick," Arthur replied.

Margaret flushed. "We're just friends."

"Or so she says," Brandon interjected. "You've been sleeping with him, haven't you?" he demanded.

"No, I have not," Margaret shouted back.

"Ahem," Arthur interrupted. "Brandon, before you

start pointing fingers, I'll ask you about your relationship with Candy Corners."

"Candy Corners?" Margaret echoed. "That can't possibly be her real name. Is she a stripper?"

Brandon's cheeks flooded with colour. "I don't know what you're talking about," he said to Arthur.

Arthur grinned at him. "I have pictures," he said in a low voice.

Brandon jumped up from his seat. "I'm not going to sit here and listen to this," he said before he rushed out of the room.

"Do you really have pictures of him with another woman?" Margaret asked.

Arthur nodded. "I was hoping I wouldn't need them. I was hoping you'd see the sense in divorcing him without needing proof that he's been unfaithful."

"We've only been married for a month," Margaret said, sounding shocked. "We've been together, travelling, for most of that time."

"But he sometimes goes out on an evening without you," Arthur said.

Margaret nodded. "And apparently when he does so, he finds himself strippers." She sat back in her seat as a single tear slid down her cheek.

"It's getting late and I'm getting tired," Arthur said. "Where is my nurse?"

"I'm here," said the pretty brunette who was standing near the door.

She rushed forwards and helped Arthur to his feet. He took a few steps towards the door and then stopped.

"I'll just add that everything I've told you about tonight has already been done. The trusts have been adjusted, and all of the paperwork is complete. Just in case anyone was thinking about slipping into my room and holding a pillow over my face tonight," he said.

"You can't be serious," John said.

Arthur shrugged. "I would imagine more people are murdered over money than anything else. I would suggest in this case, though, that it is to your advantage to keep me alive for as long as possible. Maybe, given time, I'll change my mind and change some things back to the way they were before."

He hobbled out of the room, leaving everyone staring after him.

"Where do we start?" Sarah asked John.

"I'll ring our solicitor in the morning," John replied. "I don't know what he can do, but we'll start there. The trusts are all held in various locations offshore, of course, so we may need solicitors outside of the UK as well."

"All of which will cost money," Phillip said.

"We can't survive on half of our regular income," John told him. "Especially not if we need to support Andrew and Stephanie, too."

"What's going to happen if I take a DNA test?" Andrew asked his mother.

Sarah looked at him for a moment and then shrugged. "I'm not certain," she admitted. "I did have an affair, one that my husband was well aware of at the time. He was involved with another woman and didn't mind, as long as I was discreet."

"That was how things were done in our social circle in those days," John said.

"Grandfather will change his mind," Margaret said confidently.

"And if he doesn't, both of you can help Andrew," John suggested. "If you each give Andrew a quarter of your income, you will both have half of your previous income."

"I can't live on half of my previous income," Margaret said. "Especially not if I have to get a divorce."

"And we all need to start trying for babies," Andrew added. "Not that mine will get anything if I fail my DNA test, but we need to start trying right away anyway."

Janet looked over at Rachel, who was silently crying. No one else seemed to have noticed.

"We should all get some sleep," John suggested. "Tomorrow is another day. Perhaps we'll be able to talk some sense into my father in the morning."

"The storm is getting worse," Harold said from behind the bar. "We'll take each of you back to your cottages in one of the golf carts."

They all walked into the foyer together.

"There's room for four in the cart," Harold said.

"You guys go," Phillip suggested. "Rachel and I will wait."

"Janet and I will wait, too," Edward said.

Margaret nodded. "I need to find Brandon. He has some explaining to do."

"And we need to talk and start trying to work out what we're going to do," Andrew said, taking Stephanie's hand.

The trio walked outside with Harold. Janet frowned as the wind blew into the foyer before they shut the door behind themselves.

In the sudden silence, Janet looked at Rachel.

"Are you okay?" she asked quietly.

Rachel shook her head. "Not at all."

Chapter 7

"Let's sit and chat while we wait for Harold to get back," Janet suggested.

Rachel looked as if she wanted to disagree, but after a moment, she shrugged. "Sure," she muttered as she walked over to one of the couches along the wall.

Janet joined her as Edward began a conversation with Phillip about Scotch.

"I'm not going to pry," Janet said as soon as she was next to Rachel. "But if you want a sympathetic ear, I'm here."

"Phillip and I have been trying for a baby for three years," the other woman blurted out before blushing bright red. "We haven't told anyone. I don't want sympathy."

Janet nodded. "It's difficult, isn't it? When I got married, I assumed that St. John and I would have several children. That was how it was meant to work, after all, but as the years went past, it started to seem as if it would never happen. Of course, there were fewer options in those days. St. John refused to consider adoption, and he wasn't interested in visiting a doctor to see if he was the cause of our difficulties."

"We've been talking about adopting, but we haven't given up on having our own child yet. If we do adopt, though, I'm not certain our child would be recognised by Arthur's trust. If he's prepared to disown poor Andrew, I can see him refusing to recognise an adopted child," Rachel replied, tears streaming down her face.

"You need to do what's best for you, regardless of the various trusts."

"That's easy to say, but Phillip and I have always spent every penny of his income every month. We're going to struggle to survive on seventy-five per cent of what we formerly received. I can't imagine adding the expense of children to the household."

Janet bit her tongue and counted to twenty. While she had no idea how much money was involved in the various trusts, she was fairly certain that Phillip's income was considerably more generous than what most families in the UK earned in a typical year, and that even three-quarters of that income would be more than enough to support the couple and a child or two.

"We decided, just before we came here, to take a few months out from trying," Rachel continued. "After three cycles of IVF, I'm an emotional wreck, and my body is all out of sorts. We were going to wait until after the summer to start trying again."

"That seems sensible."

"But it gives Andrew and Margaret several months' head start," Rachel replied. "If Stephanie or Margaret fall pregnant first, they'll give Arthur his first great-grandchild, and we'll lose out on the extra trust fund."

"Unless Andrew isn't really John's son."

"We have to hope."

Janet frowned.

Rachel sighed. "I don't even know what I'm saying. Andrew is wonderful, and I don't want to see him lose his trust. I just don't want him and Stephanie to have a baby before I do."

"Surely Margaret won't be trying to get pregnant, not if she's planning to divorce Brandon."

"I wonder if there's anything in the trust that requires the baby to have been born in wedlock," Rachel said thoughtfully. "That sounds as if it would be something that Arthur would demand."

"In that case, Margaret either needs to stay with Brandon or get divorced and remarried before she has a baby."

"Or she could get herself pregnant as soon as possible, and then she'd have nine months to get rid of Brandon and find someone else. Knowing her, she'd go looking for an old man with a terminal condition and marry him just to fulfill the requirements of the trust. He'd only have to live until the baby is born."

Janet stared at her, unable to imagine that people would actually behave in such a way.

"Ready?" Phillip called over as Harold walked back into the house.

"Definitely," Rachel said. She stood up and then looked at Janet. "Thank you. You've helped me clarify some things in my own head, at least."

"Good," Janet replied, mystified as to what she'd actually done.

Edward held her hand tightly as the golf cart bounced along the road that led to the cottages. Phillip and Rachel were dropped off first, and then Harold drove them to their cottage.

"This should all blow over by morning," he told them as he pulled the cart up to their front door. "Breakfast will be available in the main house between seven and eleven."

"Breakfast at eleven?" Janet asked.

Harold nodded. "Some people prefer to lie in while on their holidays."

Remembering who she was meant to be, Janet simply nodded in reply. Then she and Edward climbed out of the golf cart and rushed inside. In spite of the short distance from the cart to the door, Janet felt completely soaked by time she got inside.

"That was all sorts of horrible," she told Edward as she stood and dripped all over the entryway.

"It was pretty awful," he agreed. "I'm not certain for whom I should feel the sorriest."

"Andrew, especially if the DNA test proves that John isn't his father, but even if John is his father, it's awful that his grandfather is treating him this way."

Edward nodded. "And you have raindrops everywhere," he said, reaching out to brush some water off her cheeks. "Let's get dry and then talk."

Half an hour later, they snuggled together in the large bed. Because there was nothing between them and the sea, they'd opted to leave the curtains open so that they could watch the storm.

"I can't help but feel as if something awful is going to happen," Janet said after a loud clap of thunder.

Edward pulled her closer. "We're here because Smith suspects that something awful is going to happen. After tonight, I'm going to assume that Smith thinks that someone is going to try to kill Arthur."

"But Arthur said that the changes have already been made," Janet pointed out. "And that he might be able to be persuaded to change his mind. Surely everyone there tonight wants him to stay alive long enough to change things back to the way they were."

"Let's try to get some sleep," Edward suggested. "I'm going to attempt to talk to Arthur tomorrow. I think he's behaving very badly towards everyone, and I want to know what's behind all of it."

"It was odd," Janet said, yawning. "It's almost as if he wants them all angry with him."

"It's possible that someone else is putting ideas into his head – maybe someone who stands to benefit from the new trust arrangements."

"From what we heard, no one benefits. Aside from the as-yet unborn great-grandchild that Arthur wants, that is."

"Arthur may not have told us everything, though. It's possible, maybe even likely, that he's also set up a few other trusts, maybe establishing one for his favourite nurse or his personal assistant."

Janet frowned. "This is all more complicated than it should be. We should have been warned about the situation before we arrived."

"I'm not certain what good a warning would have done, but it might have been nice." Edward agreed. "Shall I shut the curtains now?"

"As much as I'm fascinated by the storm, I'll never sleep with them open. I'm sorry that you have to get out of the nice warm bed, though. The air conditioning is chilly."

"It is. I'm sure we can adjust it somewhere, but I'm not certain where. As for getting out of bed, well, that won't be necessary." Edward held up a small remote control. He pushed a button and blackout curtains slowly closed over the huge windows.

"Can we have that in the carriage house?" Janet asked.

She and Edward were in the process of designing their dream home in the small carriage house behind Doveby

House. The sisters had agreed that it was time for them to stop sharing a house now that they were both married. The initial plans had been lovely, but Edward kept insisting on making improvements to those plans, driving the cost higher and higher until Janet had stopped looking at the estimates. Edward was paying to convert the big empty space into their home, so Janet was happy to give him free rein to add as many additional luxuries as possible. This was the first time she'd given in to temptation and suggested something as extravagant as powered curtains, though.

Edward chuckled. "They were in my initial plan, but then you said I needed to cut the budget."

"The carriage house conversion may end up costing more than we paid for Doveby House."

"You got Doveby House for a good price."

Janet opened her mouth to argue, but she yawned instead.

"Time for sleep," Edward told her. "We'll worry about the carriage house another day."

Janet nodded and then shut her eyes. A loud crash of thunder made her jump, but a few minutes later she drifted off to sleep in spite of the storm outside.

"GOOD MORNING," Edward said when Janet opened her eyes the next morning. He was standing next to the bed, holding a coffee mug.

"Coffee?" she asked.

"Indeed. I thought you might need some."

Janet sat up and took the mug. She inhaled deeply and then took a small sip of the lovely hot drink. "Thank you."

"The storm has stopped, and it looks as if it's going to

be a lovely day. I'm going up to the main house. I'm hoping to find Arthur on his own so we can have a chat."

"I'll follow you in a few minutes."

"I'll see you soon, then."

Janet put her coffee mug down and then slowly slid across the bed. She found the remote and pushed the button, smiling happily as the curtains began to open. Bright sunlight flooded the room, making Janet regret her decision. Sighing, she got out of bed and picked up her coffee. She would admire the view after her shower when she was properly awake.

Half an hour later, she headed for the main house. In spite of wearing both sunglasses and a large hat, she still felt as if the morning was far too bright. When she arrived at the house, she paused on the doorstep. *Should I knock or just walk in?* she wondered. After a moment's hesitation, she decided that Janet Smythson would simply walk in as if she owned the place.

Luckily for her, the door was unlocked. She pushed it open and then stepped into the cool, dark interior of the house.

"Hello?" she called. "Where is everyone? I'm here for breakfast."

The drawing room where they'd had drinks the previous evening was empty. Janet continued further into the house, heading for the dining room.

"Hello?" she called again, frowning as she realised that her voice was getting quieter the more worried she became. "Hello!" she yelled loudly. Janet Smythson wasn't ever timid, especially not when she was hungry, and no one was rushing about to accommodate her needs.

"Ah, hello." Stuart Banks rushed out of the kitchen. "I was just, that is, things are a bit, um...."

"Things are a bit um?" Janet repeated.

"Mr. Thomas-Blanchard arrived earlier, and he discovered, that is, um..."

Janet frowned. *Stay in character,* she told herself firmly. "I'm not especially interested in 'um,'" she said, using her fingers to put quotation marks around the last word. "I'm here for breakfast. Two eggs, poached gently, some berries of some kind, yoghurt, and coffee, of course, please."

The man opened his mouth and then shut it again several times.

Janet stared at him. "Is there a problem?"

"I don't think I should do anything until the police arrive."

"The police? Why are the police coming? What is going on?"

"Ah, Mrs. Thomas-Blanchard, hello," Harold said as he walked into the room. "I'm afraid there's been a terrible accident. We've rung for the police. Your husband insisted on it, actually."

"An accident? My husband has had an accident?"

"No, no, not at all. No, sadly, Mr. Farnsley has had an accident, although your husband seems to believe something else. The police are on their way, regardless."

"Mr. Arthur Farnsley?" Janet checked.

"Yes, Mr. Arthur Farnsley," Harold confirmed.

"Do you not think that you should ring for a doctor?" Janet asked.

"I'm afraid it's rather too late for that," Harold replied somberly.

Janet gasped. "He's dead? What happened? What sort of accident?"

"I'm sorry, but I can't answer any of those questions. It may be best if you return to your cottage for now. There should be plenty of food in the kitchen there for you to prepare your own breakfast."

"I'm sorry? Prepare my own breakfast?" Janet said, determined to remain in character. "How am I meant to do that?"

"I'm terribly sorry, but there's nothing we can do for the moment," Harold said. "Mr. Thomas-Blanchard was quite insistent that we touch nothing at all until the police arrive."

"Please tell Mr. Thomas-Blanchard that I'm going back to the cottage and that I have quite a few things I intend to discuss with him when he returns," Janet said haughtily, turning on her heel and stomping out of the room.

She walked back down to the cottages slowly, wondering if anyone else was awake. As she strolled past the back of each of the other occupied cottages, she noted that the curtains were still drawn in every window that she could see. Her stomach rumbled loudly as she tried to decide what to do next.

"Yes, okay, breakfast," she said as she patted her tummy.

Harold hadn't been exaggerating when he'd said that her kitchen was fully stocked. Everything she could have possibly wanted for breakfast was available, including some frozen pancakes and waffles and pre-cooked bacon. After considering just about everything, Janet settled for a cup of yoghurt and an apple. After she'd finished the yoghurt, she took the apple with her as she let herself out onto the beach.

The sea air smelled salty and fresh. The sand was liberally sprinkled with pieces of driftwood and seaweed, no doubt washed ashore during the storm the previous evening. Janet walked carefully to the water's edge and then turned and began a slow stroll, taking a big bite from her apple as she went.

From the water's edge, Janet could see that the curtains in the main bedroom in the second cottage were open, but she was too far away to see into the actual room. The same was true for the first cottage in the row.

"They must all be awake, then, as it's far too bright out here for anyone to still be asleep with their curtains open," Janet said softly as she turned and began to walk back the other way. She hadn't gone far when she noticed someone on the balcony at the first cottage.

As she walked behind it, Janet waved to Rachel, who looked surprised and then waved back. The woman was wearing a robe that did little to hide her figure.

"Put some trousers on," she heard Rachel call into the cottage.

Janet blushed as she continued on her way. The curtains in the main bedroom were closed when Janet reached the fourth cottage. She kept walking down the beach, past several other cottages, noting that all the curtains in the cottages she believed were unoccupied were tightly shut.

"Well, I've learned something, even if it isn't anything useful," she said softly as she ate the last bite of her apple and turned back towards her cottage. She hadn't gone far when her mobile phone rang.

"Hello?"

"Darling, I'm so sorry," Edward said. "Something awful has happened to Arthur and, well, you know, with my background in the police, that I had to get involved."

Janet frowned. "Yes, of course," she said while her mind raced. There hadn't been anything to do with the police in Edward Thomas-Blanchard's background, she was certain of that. *What is he talking about?* she wondered.

"They're sending some men in a helicopter. They should be here in an hour or less. In the meantime, if you see anyone else, please don't mention what's happened to anyone," Edward told her.

"Of course not."

"Where are you now?"

"I'm walking on the beach behind the cottages. Harold told me they couldn't make me any breakfast, so I came back to our cottage and had some yoghurt and an apple, both of which were barely adequate, and now I'm walking by myself on a deserted beach. If I had his number, I'd have already rung Captain Jepson and insisted that he come for us immediately."

"I'm afraid we're going to have to remain on the island now until the police have concluded their investigation."

"Then they'd better hurry."

"Yes, of course."

"I assume you're remaining at the main house for now."

"I'll be here for a while, certainly."

"Then I shall continue my lonely walk until I'm too tired to care about this miserable holiday, and then I'll return to our cottage and start drinking."

"Don't drink until after you've spoken to the police."

"Why should I have to talk to the police?"

"Everyone on the island will have to speak to them. It's standard procedure."

"How do I reach Captain Jepson?"

Edward sighed. "I'm truly sorry, and I will make it up to you."

"I'm not certain that you can, but I definitely expect you to try. You can start with diamonds, a collection of them."

"Yes, dear."

The Farnsley Assignment

Edward sounded so defeated that for a moment Janet was tempted to say something to reassure him. Instead, she pushed the button to end the conversation and then dropped her mobile back into her pocket.

"Did you say something about the police?" a voice asked.

Chapter 8

Janet jumped and then looked around. Rachel was standing a few feet away, partially hidden behind a large palm tree.

"Good morning," Janet said. "How are you this morning?"

The other woman shrugged. "Phillip and I barely slept last night. We're both incredibly worried about the changes that his grandfather has made to the trusts. Phillip rang his solicitors a half-dozen times, but, of course, no one answered in the middle of the night. He's trying again now."

"I hope they can help."

"Phillip is also going to talk to his brother and sister this morning. He's hoping they can come to some sort of agreement, maybe find a way to get around what Arthur is proposing."

"Get around it?"

Rachel sighed. "Phillip is probably hoping for the impossible, but he's hoping to get his brother and sister to consent to putting together some sort of legal agreement that allows for sharing of the money in the trust that Arthur has put in place for the first great-grandchild. It's to everyone's advantage to agree, but I doubt that Andrew and Margaret will see it that way."

"Can you do that? Share the money in the trust?"

"Phillip reckons that his solicitors could find a way to make it work. They would probably not mention the trust in so many words, but make it an agreement to share any extra income that suddenly becomes available to any of them – that sort of thing, anyway."

Janet nodded. "But you don't think Andrew and Margaret will agree?"

"Andrew might, because he's probably desperate to do anything that might mean that he'll still have an income next month. Margaret will probably say no, just to be contrary. I suspect she started working on making a baby last night and will continue to keep trying while going through her divorce."

"And you think Brandon will agree to that?"

"If he won't, Margaret won't have any trouble finding willing partners. Knowing her, she won't mention that she's trying to get pregnant. She's always been fairly free with her favours, if you know what I mean. Of course, knowing that, Arthur may have put something into the trust about only accepting babies born in wedlock or some such thing. I hope Margaret thinks to check the fine print before she actually gets pregnant." The smile on her face suggested that Rachel was actually hoping the opposite.

"The storm kept Edward and me awake for much of the night," Janet said.

"We barely noticed it. As I said, Phillip was ringing his solicitors. He also rang his bank and half a dozen other people. After the first hour, I gave up trying to convince him to wait for morning and went to bed, but I couldn't sleep, not with Phillip pacing around the entire house, shouting and screaming into his mobile."

"And you've only lost a quarter of your income."

Rachel flushed. "Which is a great deal of money, actually, and I'm afraid we've been guilty of spending every penny we get every month. We were both under the impression that the trusts would remain the same for Phillip's lifetime. We even have a few debts, loans that were taken out in anticipation of our income continuing uninterrupted. It's going to take some time to sort all of that out."

"Oh, dear," Janet said.

"But didn't I hear you say something about the police?"

Janet stared at her for a moment and then shrugged. "Edward was saying something about them, but I wasn't really listening. I'm certain he was simply making excuses for why he couldn't join me on my walk."

"Where is he?"

"He went up to the main house for breakfast. I was going to join him, but I was too hungry to walk that far just for some yoghurt and fruit, which is what I typically eat in the mornings. As our cottage's kitchen was adequately stocked with such things, I helped myself and then came out for a walk."

"Phillip and I are avoiding the main house right now. Neither of us wants to see Arthur at the moment. Phillip wants his solicitor's opinion on the legality of what Arthur has done before he confronts the man. He's really hoping that he and his siblings will be able to reach some sort of agreement today as well. If they can, it will mean that we'll be less reliant on Arthur going forwards."

"Unless Arthur changes the trusts again."

Rachel frowned. "We're hoping to persuade him to

change them back to the way they used to be. Phillip started to worry last night that Arthur might get it into his head to suddenly decide to change the trust beneficiaries to some charitable groups, or maybe his favourite actor or something equally stupid. Phillip worked himself up into a horrible state, worrying about what his grandfather might do next."

"Rachel?" The voice echoed across the beach.

"I'm here," Rachel called back, stepping out of the trees and onto the beach. She waved, and a few moments later Phillip joined them.

"Ah, good morning, Mrs. Thomas-Blanchard," he said to Janet.

"You may call me Janet," she replied. "How are you today?"

He shrugged. "I've been better. The scene with my grandfather last night was unpleasant, at best. I'm eager to talk to my brother and my sister so that we can start to work out how we can deal with Grandfather's plans."

"Of course, I'm of a different generation, but I do worry about your father."

Phillip nodded. "Of course, of course. Father has been put in a difficult spot, hasn't he? I'm not certain my parents can live on half of their former income, but it isn't as if any of us will have money to spare, not now, at least not before one of us has given Grandfather a great-grandchild."

"And then that child can support us all," Rachel murmured.

"Now, now, that would hardly be fair to the little darling," Phillip countered. "He or she will be more than welcome to a share of the trusts. I just want to do everything I can to help Andrew and Margaret get through these trying times."

Of course you do, Janet thought.

A buzzing noise interrupted the conversation. Phillip pulled out his mobile and frowned at the screen. "It's a dear friend of mine," he said. "I need to take this."

As he walked away, Janet could hear the very beginning of the conversation.

"I've been ringing you for hours," Phillip complained. "My grandfather has been playing around with the family trusts. You need to stop him."

Janet mentally bleeped the four or five curse words that had been generously sprinkled into what she'd heard. Rachel made a face.

"He doesn't usually use that sort of language," she told Janet as Phillip disappeared down the beach.

"And yet he told me he wasn't all that upset about what his grandfather has done."

Rachel nodded. "I don't really understand any of this. I probably misunderstood how upset he was last night."

"I just hope everything can be resolved," Janet said.

"Yes, thank you," Rachel replied. She was staring past Janet, down the beach.

When Janet looked over, she could see Phillip waving at them.

"I think he needs me," Rachel said. "I'll see you later."

She rushed away before Janet could reply. Janet watched as Rachel joined Phillip on the sand behind their cottage. After a short conversation, the pair turned and went into the house together.

Janet returned to walking up and down the beach. After a short while, she sat down on a conveniently located bench near the water. She was about halfway along the row of cottages and had a good view of the back of all of them, in spite of the palm trees that were dotted everywhere. After sitting and watching the water for a few minutes, she turned around and sat with her back to the waves, looking instead at the row of cottages.

"What are you hoping to see?" a voice asked.

Janet jumped, and then smiled at Andrew as he crossed to her.

"I'm studying the architecture," she told him. "My first husband and I used to travel a great deal, and he was fascinated by architecture. These beach cottages are all very similar, but when you really study them, they're all different."

"Are they? I've never paid much attention. The second cottage has been mine since I turned eighteen. I remember being very excited when my grandfather gave it to me. Not that I actually own it, of course. The deed to the property is held by the trust, just like everything else on this island and in my life. Theoretically, I have millions at my disposal, but in fact I have a comfortable income that is about to come to a screeching halt."

"You don't think you'll get the necessary results from a DNA test?"

"I'm not going to take a DNA test. Stephanie and I sat up all night talking about Arthur's ridiculous demands. As long as my father is happy to accept me as his son, I don't care about the rest. Arthur can cut me off without a penny and Stephanie and I will find a way to survive." He looked at Janet and shrugged. "I may even try to find a job," he said with a small laugh.

"Did you go to uni?"

"Oh, yes, of course. Grandfather insisted on it. I have a degree in anthropology, which is useless for much of anything, but it was interesting to study. As I didn't think I was going to need to work, I chose to study what I found interesting."

"Perhaps you could teach."

"Not with just an undergraduate degree. And I can't go back to school without any money." He shook his head. "We'll be fine. Stephanie has a little bit of her own money. We'll find a way to manage. My father will help as much as he can, although I know he's going to have enough of his own worries now that Grandfather has cut his income so significantly."

"Perhaps your brother and sister will help you."

"Phillip will probably offer to help, but then find that he simply can't afford to do much. As for Margaret, I can't see her even offering. She won't want to do anything that might upset Grandfather and put her at risk of losing her own income."

"So what now?" Janet asked after a moment.

"Now I go and talk to Grandfather. If I can have five minutes of his time, I'm hoping I can persuade him to change his mind. If he wants to punish my mother for having had an affair, there are better ways to do that than to disown me. Okay, that's just my opinion, but I'm hoping to persuade other people to see it that way, too."

"I hope it all works out for you," Janet said. As soon as the words were out of her mouth, she wondered if they were in keeping with her character, but then she decided that Andrew had too much on his mind to care.

"I need to go and find Stephanie. She was going to walk up to the main house and beg for an appointment with Grandfather. She was supposed to text me if they said yes so that I could join them, but she hasn't texted or returned."

Janet nodded and then watched as the man walked away. As she tried to decide what to do next, she heard someone calling her name.

"Janet? Mrs. Tom-Blankhard, or whatever it was?"

Unable to decide if she should be offended or amused, Janet opted for amused as she smiled at Margaret.

"It's Mrs. Thomas-Blanchard, but please call me Janet," she replied as the woman sat down next to her on the bench.

"I saw you earlier, talking to Rachel, and then I saw you talking to Andrew. I suppose they've both been complaining about me," Margaret said.

"Actually, they've both been complaining about your grandfather."

Margaret laughed. "Yes, of course. I can't say as I blame them for that, although Rachel has nothing to complain about – not really, anyway. She and Phillip can survive on their reduced income. They may have to take fewer holidays, and Rachel may not get yet another diamond bracelet for their wedding anniversary this year, but otherwise, they'll be fine."

"They did seem to have been the least unfortunate last night."

Margaret stared at her for a moment and then laughed again. "The least unfortunate is a good way to put it. We were all well and truly fff, er, Grandfather treated all of us quite badly, really, but Phillip and Rachel came out better than the rest of us. No surprise there, really."

"Oh?"

"Phillip has always been Grandfather's favourite. Oh, he fussed a bit when I was born, because I was his first granddaughter, but on the whole, he has little use for women. He's been married eleven times, and I don't believe he's ever been happily married. I've been told that he loved my father's mother a great deal, but she died in an accident when my father was young."

"Perhaps all of his subsequent marriages were attempts to find that love again."

"If they were, then he definitely went looking in the wrong places." She waved a hand. "It's the same old story, really. As he got older, his wives kept getting younger until it became an embarrassment to the family and obvious to the world that the women he was marrying were only interested in his money. Most of them, sadly, were unaware of the family trust situation. If they had been, I suspect my grandfather's love life would have been a great deal less colourful."

"Surely, after the first few wives, people must have become more aware of the trust situation."

"You should look through the list of women who have been Mrs. Arthur Farnsley," Margaret suggested. "By travelling around the world and moving in and out of different social circles, my grandfather never had any difficulty in finding women who were willing to marry him. He can be charming and generous when it suits him. The women would have been given every reason to believe that he was incredibly wealthy, and he would have done nothing to correct their assumptions."

"I'm surprised your father didn't intervene."

"He did, eventually, after Grandfather's last marriage. Grandfather was seventy, and the woman in question was twenty-six. I was only a child, but I acted as flower girl for the ceremony. I remember her talking to her friends, the bridesmaids, while they were getting ready. She was laughing and bragging about how Arthur was too stupid to make her sign a prenuptial agreement and how she was going to get herself pregnant and then demand a fortune from him if he wanted to be involved in the child's life."

"My goodness."

"I told her she was wasting her time trying to scam my grandfather, but she called me a spoiled bitch and then kicked me out of the wedding party. I went and told my father what I'd heard, and he just laughed. Six months later, she was pregnant, and my grandfather divorced her."

"Even though she was pregnant?"

"It wasn't his child. He'd had a vasectomy after my father was born because he didn't want any more children. She wasn't the first of his wives to announce an unexpected pregnancy, but for my grandfather that was simply proof that the woman had been cheating. Anyway, after that episode, my father stepped in and put a stop to my grandfather's marriage-go-round."

"How?"

Margaret shrugged. "I know he stopped letting my father hire blonde women as assistants or as nurses. Apparently, Grandfather has a weakness for blondes. I believe he's also had a quiet word with a few of the women Grandfather has spent time with over the past few years, filling them in on how the trusts work and how unlikely they are to gain anything financially through their relationship with Grandfather. That's usually all it takes to send the women on their way."

"It seems as if the trusts don't work the way you all believed, though."

"And that's a matter for the solicitors to sort out. Jacob Farnsley, who was Grandfather's father, set up the trusts. He established different trusts in different countries so that he could take full advantage of different rules about how they could be established and also to evade as much tax as possible. We were always told that nothing could be done to alter the trusts. They provide a set amount of income for each family member, based on his or her connection to Jacob, but also based on how many other people are entitled to shares in the trust. My grandfather was an only child, and he chose to have only one child himself. He's never really approved of my father's decision to have three of us."

"And now he's found a way to change the provisions in the trusts."

"Or so he claims. I'm not certain that I believe him, and even if he does think he's managed to do something, I suspect the solicitors will have a lot to say about it. Unfortunately, taking the case through the courts will be costly. No doubt Grandfather is counting on none of us having enough money to fight him for the years and years that it will drag out."

"You said you don't believe him?"

"I think he's just trying to scare all of us into doing what he wants us to do."

"What does he want you to do?"

"Me? He wants me to divorce Brandon. He's convinced that Brandon is just after my money, which is probably true, but he's also fun in bed and good company, so I don't mind. It isn't as if he'll get much if we do divorce, thanks to the trusts. And, by the way, I told Brandon all about the trusts before we got married, so if he is after my money, he's not very smart about it."

Janet grinned at her. "And your grandfather wants a great-grandchild," she suggested.

"Oh, that will have been aimed at Phillip and Rachel. They've been married for four years now, and Grandfather feels it's time for them to have a baby. He doesn't know that Rachel has been struggling to get pregnant forever, but you never heard that from me."

Janet nodded. "What about Andrew?"

"Ah, poor Andrew. Grandfather has never been overly fond of Andrew. Of course, our father needed a child, but as far as Grandfather was concerned, one was enough. At least I had the good sense to be a girl, so a bit of a novelty, but Andrew is simply completely superfluous. I've no doubt that Grandfather was telling the truth about having just been given evidence that my mother cheated on my father. Mother has admitted to as much, after all. Grandfather must have been delighted when he was told, as it will give him a chance to disinherit Andrew, something he's always wanted to do. He'd be delighted to disinherit me as well, as that would keep all of the trusts together, from him to my father to Phillip, without any unnecessary complications."

Janet sighed. "It's all unfortunate, isn't it?"

"That's one word for it."

Before either woman could continue, Janet heard the sound of approaching helicopters. They both stood up and watched as three helicopters, including one that was clearly marked "Police," flew towards the island.

"It looks as if they're going to land on the other side of the island," Margaret said. "But what are they doing here?"

Chapter 9

Before Janet could reply, her mobile rang.

"Hello?"

"Darling, the police have arrived. Everyone is being asked to come up to the main house immediately," Edward told her.

"The main house?" Janet echoed.

"Yes. Harold will be ringing all of the children and inviting them."

The words were barely out of Edward's mouth when Margaret's mobile rang. She frowned at it and then answered.

"What?" she snapped.

"Now?"

"I'd rather not."

"Why are the police here?"

Janet watched as a dozen different emotions played across the other woman's face. After a moment, Margaret sighed.

"I'll wake Brandon and we'll be there soon," she said before she dropped her phone back into her pocket.

"It seems as if we're all being summoned to the main house," she said to Janet. "Something awful must have happened. The police are here."

"I hope everyone is okay," Janet said. "I'm going to go and freshen up. I'll see you at the house later."

Margaret nodded, but she was clearly distracted. She was pulling her mobile out of her pocket again as she walked back towards her cottage. Janet was tempted to follow her, to see if she could hear anything interesting in the conversation Margaret was about to have, but she also needed to get herself up to the main house without delay. While she was trying to decide what to do, Margaret tapped on her screen a few times and then put the phone away.

"She was just sending a text," Janet muttered to herself as she headed back towards her cottage. "And now I really need to hurry."

It took her only a few minutes to comb her hair and powder her nose. When she reached the main house, Harold met her at the door.

"We're asking everyone to wait in the drawing room," he said somberly.

Janet nodded and then followed him into the now-familiar room. Andrew and Stephanie were sitting on one of the couches, holding hands. They both looked at her as she walked into the room.

"Do you have any idea what's happening?" Stephanie demanded. "I came up to ask to speak to Arthur, and no one will let me see him or tell me what's going on."

Janet frowned. "My husband just rang me and asked me to come to the main house. He said it was important but refused to answer any questions. I'm not accustomed to being treated in this way. He'd better have a good explanation for all of this."

"I don't mean to be rude," Andrew said. "But why is your husband asking people to do anything on my grandfather's island?"

"I wish I knew," Janet replied angrily.

"Andrew, Stephanie," Phillip said as he walked into the room. "I was hoping I could speak to both of you later."

"Of course," Andrew said. "I think we have a lot to discuss, actually."

Phillip nodded and then sat down on the couch opposite Andrew. "I'm sorry for the way that Grandfather is treating you," he said.

Andrew shrugged. "At least Father is standing by me – for now, anyway."

"And I will continue to stand by you, whatever my father seems to think," John said as he strode into the room. Sarah was a few paces behind him. "But what is this nonsense? Janet, where is Edward? Don't tell me he's been dragged into something?"

"I've no idea what is going on," Janet replied.

John sighed and then dropped heavily into a chair. "Whatever it is, it can't be more horrible than the scene over dinner last night. That was appalling on every possible level."

Sarah sat down next to him and took his hand. "We'll find a way through this in the same way we've muddled through every other challenge life has thrown at us."

John smiled and then sighed again. "But in the past, we've always had an adequate income with which to tackle our problems. With our income halved, I'm not certain what we'll do."

"We'll work it out," Sarah said confidently.

"Am I late?" Rachel asked as she hurried into the room. "I was soaking in a hot bath when Harold rang. I thought it might help with all the stress, but then I had to hurry to get here and now I'm feeling even more stressed than I was when I ran the bath."

"Sorry, darling," Phillip said. "I shouldn't have made it sound so urgent, but Harold sounded upset when he rang. Margaret and Brandon aren't here yet, though, so you needn't have rushed."

"We're here," Margaret announced from the doorway.

She walked into the room, dragging Brandon behind her. It was obvious that he'd only just woken up. To Janet it looked as if he was still wearing a pyjama shirt, but at least he'd pulled on proper trousers. Janet had to swallow a laugh when she noticed that he was wearing bedroom slippers.

"Grandfather isn't going to approve of those slippers," Phillip said.

Margaret shrugged. "Brandon couldn't find his shoes this morning. He walked back to the cottage in the rain, so his shoes were soaked. He left them on the covered patio to dry, rather than wear them into the cottage and ruin the floors. They weren't there when we were ready to come out."

"Maybe the wind blew them away," Stephanie suggested.

"I doubt it, but maybe," Margaret replied. "He only brought the one pair, though, so we need to find them."

"I'll help you look after lunch," Rachel offered. "I hope we won't have to dig through the sand to find them."

The door opened, and the island's staff filed into the room. Janet smiled at Harold, Stuart, and Sammy as she studied the two women she'd not yet had the chance to meet. From their pictures, Dawn Becker and Audrey Fowler had looked very similar, but in person the resemblance was less noticeable. They were both brunettes and around the same height and weight, but Dawn looked older, and Janet thought she looked tired as well.

It had been Audrey who had been with Arthur the previous evening. She was frowning, and Janet thought she looked as if she'd been crying. Dawn looked more as if she'd just woken up for the day. The women were meant to be providing round-the-clock care for Arthur, though, so perhaps Dawn had been up all night, or at least for part of it.

While Janet was thinking, three more men had walked into the room. The oldest appeared around forty-five, with dark hair that was starting to go grey. He was taller than the other two men, and, as he walked to the centre of the room, he seemed to be studying everyone around him. The other two men were probably in their thirties. One was blonde, and the other had dark hair. They both stood in the doorway staring straight ahead with blank expressions on their faces. Edward had followed them into the room. He gave Janet a reassuring smile and then joined the older man in the room's centre.

"Thank you all for coming," the tallest man said after a moment. "I'm Inspector Joe Price. I'm a police inspector, and I've been given jurisdiction over the investigation into the unexplained death of Mr. Arthur Farnsley."

A few people gasped while Brandon started to laugh.

"He's dead? The grumpy old ba, er, villain is dead? Maybe now I'll be able to stay married," he said. "Have you inherited a fortune?" he asked Margaret.

She frowned at him. "Hush," she said quietly.

"Was he murdered?" Andrew asked.

Inspector Price stared at him for a moment before replying. "That's not for me to decide. It could be several days before we have the results of the postmortem."

"Several days?" John echoed. "I need to get back to London."

"I'm afraid everyone is going to have to remain on the island for the time being," the inspector countered. "As with any unexplained death, we're treating this as a murder investigation until such time as we're told otherwise."

"So he was murdered," Stephanie said.

"Again, it isn't my job to determine that," the inspector replied.

"Who found the body?" Phillip asked.

"I did," Edward replied. "I came up to the house this morning specifically to speak to Arthur. I had a business proposition I wanted to put to him, but when I arrived here, Harold told me that Arthur was still in bed. I, well, I'm afraid I rather insisted on seeing him, and after some considerable effort, I was able to persuade Harold to allow me to knock on Arthur's door."

"Where was his nurse?" Sarah demanded. "He's meant to have a nurse with him at all times."

"I was in my room," Audrey replied. "Dawn worked the night shift, but she finished at seven. I was meant to wake Mr. Farnsley at eight."

"And Father died between seven and eight?" John asked.

"That has yet to be determined," the inspector told him.

"Either he died between seven and eight, or someone didn't do her job properly last night," John said angrily.

Dawn flushed. "I helped get him ready for bed, and then I sat with him until he fell asleep. After that, my job was simply to be available if I was needed. Mr. Farnsley had a button to push if he wanted me, so I was able to go back to my room and rest unless he pushed the button. Audrey does the same when she's working the night shift."

Audrey nodded. "Mr. Farnsley doesn't, or rather, didn't want to be disturbed when he was sleeping, which meant that we didn't typically check on him once he'd fallen asleep. He knew to press his button if he needed us."

"And how often did he need you?" Janet asked.

Dawn frowned. "Every bloody night," she snapped before sighing. "I am sorry," she said. "I was able to rest last night, but I rarely manage to sleep when I'm on duty because I'm always expecting the buzzer to go off at any moment. I spent much of last night pacing back and forth in my room, listening to the storm. I'd only just crawled into bed when I was woken up and asked to come here for this."

Audrey patted her arm. "Mr. Farnsley used to suffer from insomnia. When he had difficulty falling asleep, he would ring for one of us and then want to talk until he felt tired enough to try to sleep again. I learned a long time ago that it was safer to stay awake, in case I was needed, than to fall asleep and then get dragged out of that sleep."

"So, what happened when you knocked on his door this morning?" John asked Edward.

"I knocked, and I thought I heard someone reply," Edward told him. He shrugged and looked a bit sheepish. "Obviously, I was mistaken, but when I thought I'd heard a reply, I opened the door to the bedroom. It was immediately obvious that something was wrong. I've had some experience with police investigations in the past, so I rang a colleague of mine, and he put things into motion to get Inspector Price here."

"You've had experience with police investigations?" Phillip asked. "What does that mean?"

"I don't think we need to question Edward about his

past right now," John said. "My father, your grandfather, is dead."

There was a long silence. Sarah buried her head on her husband's shoulder while a few tears trickled down Rachel's face. Eventually, Margaret sighed.

"So now what?" she asked. "You said we're stuck here?" she asked the inspector.

"We're asking everyone to remain on the island until the initial investigation is complete," he replied. "That includes getting the results of the postmortem examination."

"What about the trusts?" Margaret asked. "What happens to them?"

"That's a very good question," her father replied. "What should happen is that my father's share of the trust becomes mine, and the share that I was receiving gets divided among my three children and added to the shares that they already receive. After last night, though, I've no idea what happens now."

"We need to talk to Grandfather's solicitor," Margaret said.

"I can take care of that," Harold offered. "Having served as Mr. Farnsley's assistant for many years, I'm well aware of the many legal representatives he used."

"We'll talk later," John told him. "I suspect we're going to need your help in a lot of areas."

Harold nodded. "Very good, sir," he said.

"I hope we have enough food and supplies for an extended stay," John said.

Harold looked at Sammy. "The island is your concern," he said.

Sammy grinned. "No one will starve to death in the next week," he said. "You may not all get exactly what you want for every meal, but there should be enough food in your cottages to keep you all fed for a while."

"In our cottages?" Margaret repeated.

"Of course, Stuart will be preparing meals in the main house for anyone who would prefer to eat here," Harold said quickly.

Stuart nodded. "The kitchen here is fully stocked with plenty of food for a week. I can order more supplies if it seems as if we'll be here longer."

"Surely I don't need to be here," Janet interjected. "I'm terribly sorry to hear about Mr. Farnsley's untimely death, but I didn't even know the man."

"Unfortunately, because you were on the island when he died, we're going to have to ask you to remain here until we've completed our initial investigation," the inspector told her.

Janet frowned. "Edward, do something. I don't want to stay here."

"We'll talk later," Edward replied. "It's fine."

"It is not fine," Janet countered, almost enjoying being rude and difficult. "You promised me an incredible holiday cruising around the Bahamas. Being stuck on a tiny island with a murderer wasn't in the plans."

"Now, now," John said. "No one here is a murderer."

Margaret laughed. "Daddy, darling, the police are here because they think Grandfather was murdered. If they're correct, then someone in this room killed him."

John looked around the room and then focussed his attention on Margaret. "That simply isn't possible. If my father was murdered, then he must have been killed by someone who sneaked onto the island in the middle of the night."

"During that storm last night?" Margaret asked. "Impossible."

"Maybe someone arrived before the storm and has been hiding somewhere on the island," John said rather desperately. "The police should be out there looking for our uninvited guest before he or she escapes."

"There are only two docks on the island, and there are boats tied up in both of them," Harold pointed out. "It's almost impossible to get access to the island any other way."

"Almost, but not entirely," John said. "Someone may have simply sailed close to the island and then swum the rest of the way."

Harold opened his mouth and then shut it again. He looked at the inspector and shrugged. "Anything is possible," he said in a low voice.

"We'll be searching the island for anyone who doesn't belong here," Inspector Price said. "We have a patrol boat circling the island so that we can be certain that no one comes or goes during our investigation."

"But the killer has had all night to get away," John argued. "The storm was over by four, which gave him or her several hours to escape."

"I can assure you that we'll be considering all possibilities," Inspector Price replied. "For now, though, the first thing that I need to do is talk to each of you individually. I need to get your statements on everything that's happened in the past twenty-four hours."

"Yawn," Margaret said. "You're going to get a dozen different versions of the big family fight that we had last night. I can summarise it for you, though. Grandfather was being horrible and upset all of us. We all went to bed angry and eager to talk to Grandfather again this morning to try to change his mind. None of us wanted him dead, because now it's too late to change his mind."

"Maybe he was lying about having already made all of the changes," Stephanie said hopefully.

"We can hope," John muttered.

"Harold has kindly offered me the use of a small office here, on the ground floor," Inspector Price said. "I'll be using that throughout the course of the investigation. I'll be giving each of you one of my cards when we speak, but I expect to be in that office for much of every day. If you need to speak with me, feel free to try to find me there before you ring my mobile number."

"How much longer will this take?" Dawn asked. "I'm sorry, but I'm exhausted."

"Why don't you go back to your room and get some sleep?" the inspector suggested. "I can take your statement when you wake up later in the day."

"It will probably be much later," she warned the man as she stood up.

"That's fine. I'd rather speak to you when you're well rested," he replied.

Dawn nodded and then turned and left the room. As she disappeared down the corridor, one of the two men in the doorway turned and followed her.

"Mr. Parker, I'm going to start with you, please," Inspector Price said.

Harold looked surprised, but then he nodded and got to his feet.

"I will ask the rest of you to remain here. I'll speak to each of you in turn. While you are welcome to chat amongst yourselves, Tommy will be listening to your conversations, so please speak up."

Tommy, the policeman in the doorway, smiled brightly as Harold and Inspector Price left the room together.

"This is crazy," Margaret said to Brandon. "We're

actually suspects in a murder investigation. It's something off the telly."

"You do understand that Grandfather is dead, don't you?" Andrew asked. "I can't quite get my head around it."

"It's awful," Sarah said, lifting her head from John's shoulder. "He was as much a father to me as my own father."

John chuckled. "To be fair, that isn't saying much," he said.

Sarah stiffened. "Now is not the time to start reminding me of my horrible childhood," she said angrily.

"You brought it up," John countered.

"I'm too upset about the tragic loss of my father-in-law to even speak to you," Sarah replied as she sat up and slid several inches away from John.

He put a hand on her shoulder. "I didn't mean to upset you. I've just lost my father, and I'm too upset to even think straight."

"Be careful when you talk to the police," Brandon warned him. "You don't want to end up at the top of the list of suspects."

"I'm not a suspect," John replied dismissively.

"We're all suspects," Margaret countered. "Of course, we all wanted Grandfather alive, which means none of us had a motive, but we're still going to be suspects, regardless."

"Did we all want Grandfather alive?" Stephanie asked. "Phillip didn't have much to complain about after last night, and I'm sure he was as worried as the rest of us that Grandfather might make even more changes to things in the future."

Phillip opened his mouth to reply, but John held up a hand. "We are not going to start throwing around hurtful and unnecessary accusations," he said firmly. "It's entirely possible that my father died of natural causes and that this entire police investigation is a waste of time. Regardless, we are a family, and we will continue to support one another forever." He looked around the room slowly. "Forever!" he repeated after a moment.

Stephanie looked as if she wanted to argue, but instead she sat back in her seat and began to pick at her nail polish.

"What's for lunch?" Andrew asked Stuart several minutes later.

"I've no idea," he replied flatly. "Mr. Farnsley always chose the day's menu when he came down for breakfast. I was still waiting for him to arrive to do so when I was told that he'd passed away. I suppose I'll have to talk to Mr. Parker in order to prepare today's menus."

"We could all discuss the options and vote on our favourites," Rachel suggested.

Stuart shook his head. "I'm quite certain that Mr. Parker will want to determine the menus."

"Or I could do it," Sammy suggested. "I'm responsible for ordering the supplies, after all."

"We'll have to discuss it once we've all finished with the police," Stuart replied.

"By that time, you'll need to discuss dinner, not lunch," Stephanie said. "And some of us haven't had breakfast yet, actually."

Janet had had breakfast, but she was starting to get hungry again. It was nearly midday, and it seemed likely that Stephanie was correct. The police were probably not going to finish speaking to everyone until the evening.

When the inspector had left the room, Edward had followed him to the door and then stopped and stood in the corner of the room. Janet tried not to stare at him, as she suspected that he was hoping to be almost unnoticed there, but she frequently found herself looking in his direction. While everyone had been talking, he'd clearly been paying attention, but now he pulled one of his little brown notebooks out of his pocket and began to make notes.

Janet sighed and shifted in her seat. A moment later, the inspector appeared in the doorway with a young man in a blue police uniform.

"This is Jake," the inspector told them. "He's going to be collecting each of you in turn and escorting you to my office." He said something to Jake and then turned and walked away.

After a moment, Jake looked around the room and then spoke. "Mr. Banks? The inspector is ready for you now."

Stuart jumped up. "I'll try to persuade him to let me get started on lunch as soon as we're done speaking," he told everyone as he headed for the door. "Mr. Farnsley didn't approve of people eating in here, but maybe the inspector will allow you all to move into the dining room once lunch is ready."

"I hope so," John said. "If nothing else, for a change of scenery."

"I'm not hungry," Sarah replied. "I don't feel as if I'm ever going to want to eat again."

The room lapsed into another awkward silence.

Chapter 10

As the time ticked past slowly, Janet amused herself by trying to guess the order in which the inspector would interview everyone. Since he'd started with the staff, she assumed that Sammy would be next, and she was correct. Then she guessed that he'd talk to Audrey before starting on the family, but after Sammy, John was the next to be called. After John, the inspector sent for Sarah. She'd only just left the room when Stuart appeared in the doorway.

"If anyone is hungry, I have everything ready in the kitchen for you to put together your own sandwiches. The inspector has agreed that you can all move into the kitchen and then into the dining room to eat," he announced.

Janet was one of the first to her feet. It wasn't so much that she was hungry, it was more that she was bored. The tension in the room had been mounting all afternoon as well, and she was hoping the change in scenery might help diffuse some of that.

Stuart led them all into the kitchen. Janet's mouth watered as she looked at the large trays that were spread across the huge island at the centre of the room. One held various types of bread rolls and sliced bread. A second was filled with thickly sliced ham, turkey, and roast beef. Next came a variety of lettuce leaves with onion and tomato slices. Small pots held several different condiments. Bowls filled with different salads rounded out the selections.

"I'm not hungry," Rachel said flatly.

"Neither am I, but I'm going to eat," Phillip replied. "It may be a while before we get another chance."

"You say that as if you're afraid you might be arrested," Margaret said as she pushed past everyone to grab a plate.

"If anyone should be worried, it should be Brandon," Phillip shot back.

"What did I do?" Brandon asked.

"Where are your shoes?" Phillip asked pointedly.

Brandon looked down at his slippers and shrugged. "I left them on the patio at our cottage. Someone must have taken them."

"Or maybe you wore them back to the house when you came back in the middle of the night to kill Grandfather," Phillip countered. "Maybe you stepped in so much blood that you had to abandon your shoes with the body."

"Phillip!" Margaret snapped. "That's quite enough. Brandon didn't kill Grandfather. Why are you so certain there was a lot of blood around the body? Maybe he was strangled, or someone held a pillow over his face. It sounds as if you know far too much about what happened to Grandfather."

Phillip flushed. "I was just offering one possible explanation for what happened," he replied. "I simply can't imagine why anyone would have stolen Brandon's shoes."

"Unless there is someone on the island who doesn't belong," Stephanie said. "Maybe that someone killed your grandfather and stole Brandon's shoes."

"I think that seems highly unlikely," Phillip replied. "The family has owned Farntopia since before I was born. To the best of my knowledge, we've never had any intruders in the past."

"That's something to ask Sammy about," Andrew suggested.

"Farntopia is a dumb name," Margaret said.

"I think we can all agree on that," Phillip replied.

"Where did the name come from?" Janet asked as she finally stepped forwards and began to fill her plate. After Margaret had made her sandwich, the others had all simply stood and stared at the food until Janet couldn't take it any longer.

"One of Grandfather's wives named it," Andrew told her. "They spent their honeymoon here, although that wasn't unusual. Grandfather almost always spent his honeymoons here."

"It's a wonderful place for that," Phillip said. "Rachel and I had a brilliant fortnight here right after our wedding."

"It's very romantic," Stephanie agreed. "When Andrew and I came for our honeymoon, I never wanted to leave."

"Grandfather wouldn't let me bring Humphrey here," Margaret complained. "And then, when I married Brandon, he refused to let us come as well. He said something about Farntopia being for honeymoons for first marriages, which made me laugh, because he'd brought at least five or six of his wives here."

"But it was his island, so he got to make the rules," Phillip said.

"Says the man who never had to deal with any of Grandfather's completely unfair rules," Margaret muttered under her breath.

The Farnsley Assignment

"The inspector is ready for Mr. Phillip Farnsley," Jake said in the doorway.

Phillip frowned at the empty plate in his hand. "I haven't had lunch yet," he complained.

"Why don't you make yourself a sandwich and take it with you?" Jake suggested.

Janet took her very full plate and walked to the table in the corner of the room. She sat down and then took a bite of her sandwich. As she chewed, she realised that she didn't have any silverware, which meant she wouldn't be able to eat her salads. Before she could do anything to rectify the situation, Edward joined her at the table. He didn't have any food, but he was carrying two sets of utensils wrapped in cloth napkins. He set them on the table and then winked at Janet.

"Thanks," she said after she'd swallowed.

"I'll be right back," he replied.

"So tell us about your connection to the police," Andrew demanded as Edward walked back to the counter to fill a plate.

Edward chuckled. "I'm afraid I can't do that," he said.

"What does that mean?" Stephanie asked.

"Can't or won't?" Margaret added.

"Can't," Edward said seriously. "The Official Secrets Act and all of that."

"I don't believe it," Brandon said. "You just don't want to tell us anything. Maybe you're a convicted killer. Maybe the police should be looking more closely at where you were last night."

Edward shrugged. "I've never been convicted of anything," he said in a tone that suggested that the key word in the sentence was convicted. "And I'm quite certain that I'm as much a suspect in the investigation as anyone else."

"Not me," Janet said loudly from her seat. "I didn't even know the poor man."

"You're still a suspect, my darling," Edward told her as he walked back towards her with a plate piled high with food. "We'll all be suspects if the postmortem finds that Arthur was murdered, right up until the police find the killer."

"I refuse to allow myself to be a suspect," Janet said. "I should have rung my solicitor by now, shouldn't I?"

"Actually, we should all insist on having solicitors with us when we speak to the police," Andrew said.

"But that just makes you look guilty," Margaret argued.

"It's a sensible precaution," Andrew retorted. "I'm not going to speak to the inspector without my solicitor present."

"Your solicitor is in London," Stephanie pointed out. "We may be about to be disinherited. Now isn't the time to be paying a fortune to fly that man here."

"Not unless you're guilty," Margaret added.

Andrew frowned. "But we're entitled to representation. Maybe I could find a local solicitor who could help."

"We can't afford anything right now," Stephanie said flatly. "If you're cut off, we'll have to rely on my money, and I can tell you right now that I'm not going to be paying for a solicitor to come and hold anyone's hand during police questioning. If you say something stupid and get yourself arrested, we'll talk."

Andrew frowned. "I love you, too," he said sharply.

Stephanie smiled. "This isn't about love. This is about having enough money to pay our mortgage next month and the month after that. We've never had to worry about money before, but we may have to worry about it a great deal going forwards. Since we're now talking about my money, I'll be the one making the final decisions on what we spend."

"Mrs. Rachel Farnsley? The inspector is ready for you," Jake said from the doorway.

As Rachel left the room, some of the others filled plates and then moved into the dining room. After a few minutes, only Janet and Edward and Audrey were left in the kitchen.

"This is awkward," Audrey said after she'd filled her plate. "I'm not family, but you're guests of the family. I can't take this back to my room, though."

"You're welcome to join us," Edward told her. As he smiled at the pretty nurse, Janet shot him an angry look.

"Sit here, next to me," she suggested, patting the chair next to hers. "Edward, did I see something up there for pudding?" she asked.

Edward frowned and then stood up. "I didn't see anything for pudding," he said.

"Perhaps you could find out if there is anything, then," Janet suggested.

"Of course, darling," he said before he turned and left the room.

"I don't entirely trust him," Janet told Audrey in a confiding tone. "Men are prone to cheating, aren't they?"

"Yes, of course," Audrey replied. "I'd never get involved with a married man, though."

"Very good, dear." Janet patted her arm. "Of course, with what you do, I'm sure you've had to deal with a lot of improper suggestions over the years."

Audrey nodded. "It can get quite awkward, but you learn how to handle it, or you find a different line of work."

"Did you always want to be a nurse?"

"My mother fell ill when I was ten," Audrey replied.

"She was in and out of hospital every few months until she finally passed away when I was thirteen. One of the nurses who'd helped look after my mother for those years had become almost like family to me. After my mother died, she took me in. I didn't have anyone else."

"Where was your father?"

Something flashed over Audrey's face before she shrugged. "I'm not sure. But Nurse Gloria, she treated me as if I was the daughter she'd never had. She was the one who encouraged me to study nursing. It seemed the best way to honour my mother's memory and pay tribute to the woman who'd raised me after my mother's death."

"What made you decide to start doing private nursing, then?"

"Money," Audrey said flatly.

Someone laughed. Janet looked up and smiled at Dawn as she walked into the kitchen.

"She's right. The money is a lot better in private nursing," Dawn said. "I worked in one of the biggest hospitals in the UK, and the pay was terrible. I was working sixty or seventy hours a week, dealing with thirty or forty patients at a time, and struggling to make ends meet. One of my friends quit and took a private job, and a year later, she was driving a brand-new car and moving into a bigger flat. I thought I'd try it for a year myself and see if I could do it or not, and here we are."

"When is your year up?" Janet asked.

Dawn laughed again. "Three years ago. After the first year, I realised that the money was too good to give up, so here I am. This is one of the best jobs I've ever had, or it was until last night. Mr. Farnsley was very generous and not terribly demanding."

"It was better when we were in London or New York,"

Audrey interjected. "He had more staff there, so we worked shorter shifts."

"Yeah, but we were both quick enough to volunteer to come down here with him," Dawn said. "We're on bonus pay for the entire time we're here, and we get extra holiday time when we get back to London as well. At least, that was what was supposed to happen."

"All bets are off now," Audrey said.

Dawn nodded. "I went back to my room and started thinking about what a mess this all is, and then I couldn't sleep. I decided that, since I'll be able to sleep tonight, I should probably just get up for the day."

"We won't have any trouble finding new jobs once we get back to the UK," Audrey said confidently.

"We just have to get back to the UK," Dawn replied gloomily. "What if the family doesn't want to pay for our flights back?"

"You didn't get return tickets?" Janet asked.

"We arrived on a private jet," Dawn explained. "Mr. Farnsley always travelled by private jet."

"I'm sure the family won't just leave you here," Janet said.

"Not on the island, of course, but what if they leave us in Nassau or Miami?" Dawn asked. "I've no idea what it costs to fly to the UK, but I'm sure it's expensive."

"I can help," Audrey said quietly. "I've put nearly everything I've earned over the past few years into the bank. Since I've been living with my patients, I've had virtually no living expenses. I can buy plane tickets for both of us, and you can pay me back later."

Dawn grinned at her. "Thank you. I wish I could say that I've been saving every penny, but I've been too busy taking luxury holidays in between assignments."

"Is it possible that Mr. Farnsley died of natural causes?" Janet asked when the other two women fell silent. "Was he feeling poorly last night when he went to bed?"

Audrey shook her head. "He was quite pleased with himself, really, because he'd upset everyone. He'd been planning that conversation for the past month or so, from what I overheard."

Dawn nodded. "He started talking to his solicitors in February, I believe. One of his friends had found a loophole in a trust that had been set up on his behalf, and he'd told Mr. Farnsley all about it. I remember how excited Mr. Farnsley was after dinner that night. He told me that he was going to find his own damned loophole and exploit the, um, heck out of it."

"For a few weeks, it seemed as if he had solicitors at the house every day, first in London and then in New York," Audrey said. She looked at Dawn and then sighed. "And then he told us to start telling people that his memory was going," she added in a whisper.

"Did you tell the police that part?" Dawn asked. "I wasn't certain whether I should or not."

"I haven't had my turn with them yet," Audrey replied. "But I will tell them — when I get the chance. It could be important."

"It was just Mr. Farnsley wanting to upset everyone," Dawn suggested. "He wanted them all to think that he was struggling so that they'd come to the island this weekend."

"They would have come anyway," Audrey said. "They all always did exactly as they were told."

"Margaret, er, Mrs. Rogers sometimes fought back," Dawn retorted. "She used to ring Mr. Farnsley and have huge fights with him. Mr. Farnsley didn't approve of either of her husbands."

"But she still would have come this weekend," Audrey

insisted. "She loves the island, and she'd never pass up a chance to come here."

"Who can blame her?" Dawn asked. "Even though I'm here to work, I love it here. My bedroom may be small, but it has amazing views of the sea and the beach. I never had that when I worked in hospitals."

"It is lovely here," Audrey agreed.

"So, there wasn't anything wrong with Mr. Farnsley?" Janet asked.

The two women exchanged glances.

"He was ninety, with arthritis and several other problems associated with age," Dawn told her. "But there wasn't anything wrong with his mind. His memory was still sharp, and he was perfectly capable of looking after his various concerns."

"And he was still both able and happy to do what he could to upset his family," Audrey added. "He took perverse pleasure in upsetting everyone."

"Why?" Janet wondered.

Both women shrugged.

"I think he simply found it amusing," Dawn said after a moment. "He was born into a fabulously wealthy family to parents who didn't trust him with money. They set up all the complicated trusts on his behalf before they died, leaving him with nothing to do but sit back and collect his income for the rest of his life. I believe he could have been a very successful businessman, but he never had any reason to work. I think he tried to stave off boredom by setting his family members against one another and then sitting back and watching the fireworks."

"How awful," Janet said.

"I think, if he'd have found a way around the trusts earlier, he would have made all of the grandchildren go out and get jobs," Dawn said. "He told me once that they were all great disappointments to him because all they'd ever done is live their lives the same way he'd lived his."

"What about John?" Janet wondered.

"He started his own business after he finished uni," Audrey told her. "It was moderately successful, but after a few years he sold it to a friend and then used the proceeds to take his new wife on an extended holiday. Mr. Farnsley didn't approve. I've been told that they had a huge row and that the younger Mr. Farnsley told his father that he could quite happily just sit on his, um, bottom and do nothing for the rest of his life if his father was going to complain about how he spent his money."

"And that's just what he did," Janet guessed.

Audrey nodded. "He'd received an increase in his share of the trust when he'd married, and he got additional increases for each child, so he settled in and began to spend every penny he received and never worked another day in his life."

"You know more about the family than I do," Dawn said.

"I worked the night shift a great deal over the last year," Audrey told her. "When Mr. Farnsley couldn't sleep, he'd start telling me stories about the family. He used to ask me where he'd gone wrong with his son and with the grandchildren. Of course, I had my own opinions, but I never offered them to Mr. Farnsley."

"I would have," Janet said tartly. "He made quite a few mistakes, as far as I can see."

Audrey and Dawn both laughed.

"Do you have children?" Dawn asked.

"No, I, er..." Janet stopped and took a deep breath. "I have two adults who would be livid if I called them children," she said, trying to save the situation and her cover.

Chapter 11

"Ms. Audrey Fowler?" Jake said from the doorway. "The inspector is ready for you now."

Janet blew out a relieved sigh as Audrey followed the man out of the room.

"My mother still calls me her baby," Dawn said. "She says I'll always be her baby."

Janet shrugged. "Of course I adored my children, but I had other responsibilities. My husband, St. John, was a very successful businessman who needed a wife who could drop everything to accommodate his needs. He attended hundreds of social events each year, everything from charity fundraisers to dinners with government officials. The children had nannies and never missed me."

Dawn opened her mouth and then shut it again. After a moment, she tried again. "Do you see them often?"

"See who? Oh, my children? I haven't seen either of them in a while," Janet answered vaguely. "St. John wasn't overly fond of them. He found them noisy and demanding."

"Even as adults?"

Janet frowned. "I'm not certain he spent much time with them once they were adults. We sent them to boarding school, of course, once they were old enough. Wolf used to come home for odd holidays, but Ermine preferred to spend her holidays with friends."

"Ermine?" Dawn repeated.

"Ms. Becker? The inspector will see you now," Jake said from the doorway.

As the pair left the room, Janet sighed again and sat back in her chair. While she was enjoying the challenge of being Mrs. Janet Smythson Thomas-Blanchard, she was also finding it incredibly difficult to remember to be nasty and rude and demanding. As she reached for her teacup, Edward walked back into the room carrying a covered tray.

"What do you have there?" Janet asked.

Edward grinned at her. "What you demanded: pudding."

He put the tray down on the table and whisked away the cover. Janet could only stare at the selection of tiny puddings he'd revealed.

"Stuart loves to make puddings, but no one in the Farnsley family really enjoys them," Edward told her. "So he makes them for the staff, mostly. I found him in the staff kitchen, putting together trays for Sammy and Harold. He was happy to put one together for us as well."

"I wish I hadn't eaten such a large sandwich," Janet said as she studied the choices.

"The servings are all very small. Even if you try one of everything, it probably won't add up to a full pudding."

"Only one of everything?" Janet muttered as she began to pile her selections onto her plate.

Half an hour later, she pushed her empty plate away. "I'm too full to move," she complained.

"Everything was delicious, though."

"Except the lemon tart. It was more bitter than I like."

"I thought it was perfect."

"Maybe I married the wrong man."

Edward frowned. "If you thought it was too bitter, you're probably correct," he said quickly.

Before Janet could reply, Jake appeared in the doorway.

"Mrs. Thomas-Blanchard, the inspector is ready for you. Mr. Thomas-Blanchard, you should probably come along."

"I was thinking about ringing my solicitor," Janet said as she got to her feet. "Do you think I need to do so?" she asked Edward.

"Not at all," Edward replied.

Janet shrugged. "I'm fairly certain he wouldn't agree with you."

Jake led them down a long corridor to a room at the very end. He knocked once and then opened the door before stepping back to let Janet walk in first. Edward followed her, and then Jake walked in and shut the door behind them.

"Have a seat," the inspector suggested, gesturing towards the comfortable-looking chairs in front of the large wooden desk that he was sitting behind.

"Thank you," Janet said as she slid into a chair.

Edward took the seat next to her as Jake walked behind the desk and sat down next to the inspector.

"I'm sorry that you were kept waiting," Inspector Price began. "But I was hoping you might learn something interesting from the others while you waited."

"I don't know that I learned anything interesting, but I did have a chance to talk to a few people," Janet said.

"Let's do this right," he replied. "Start at the very

beginning, when Mr. Jones interrupted your New York City holiday and asked you to take this assignment."

Janet looked at Edward, who smiled.

"Joe has connections to the agency," he explained.

What does that mean? Janet wondered.

"And when Edward rang me and told me that you'd been sent here by Smith, I very nearly found an excuse to avoid being put in charge of the investigation," the inspector told Janet.

"I just hope Smith didn't send us here to protect Mr. Farnsley," Janet admitted.

"He didn't," Edward assured her. "I talked to Mr. Jones while I was waiting for Joe to arrive. Smith wasn't happy to hear about Arthur's untimely demise, but we're to remain here and remain vigilant."

"What does that mean?" Janet demanded.

Edward sighed and then shrugged. "I wish I knew."

"I'm not especially interested in Smith's concerns," the inspector said. "I need to investigate a murder."

"It was definitely murder?" Janet asked.

The man hesitated and then nodded. "I imagine Edward will tell you everything once you're finished here, anyway. It was definitely murder."

Janet sighed. "That poor man."

"I'm not certain that many in his family are mourning the loss," Edward said.

"He was rather horrible to them all yesterday," Janet said. "But it seems as if they would all be better off if he were still alive."

"Start at the beginning," the inspector suggested.

Janet sat back in her seat and shut her eyes. "Edward and I had stopped for a drink at a quiet little bar in New York City," she began. "And then it was finally my turn to speak to you, Inspector Price," she eventually concluded as she opened her eyes and sat up.

"Call me Joe," he said. "Maybe not in front of the Farnsley family, but we are all working on the same side."

"I may just keep calling you Inspector Price so that I don't forget and call you Joe in front of someone else," Janet replied.

He nodded. "We wouldn't want the family to think that Janet Smythson Whatever is getting special treatment," he said with a laugh.

"Now that you have Janet's statement, we can start talking about the case," Edward said.

Joe nodded. "We know that Mr. Farnsley was alive and well when he went upstairs with his nurse, Audrey. According to her statement, she helped him change into his pyjamas and brush his teeth and then helped him into bed. She keeps meticulous notes, and according to those, she turned off his light and shut his door at eleven-fourteen."

"And Edward found the body before eight," Janet said.

"Edward found the body at seven forty-three," Joe told her. "And there isn't anyone on the island who can account for his or her whereabouts for the entire evening. Of course, everyone insists that they were tucked up in their cottage or in their room, but none of that can be proven."

"Was the door to the main house locked?" Janet asked.

"Sammy claims to have locked it after his nightly walk-through of the property, which he told me he completed around midnight," Joe replied. "Harold claims that he always checks all of the doors before he goes to bed and that he found the front door unlocked around one o'clock. He locked it before he went up to bed."

"So the killer had to have sneaked in before one o'clock?" Janet asked.

"If he or she came in through the front door. There are six different entrances to the main house, though, and when I arrived, I found all six unlocked. Regardless of who checked which doors when, the sliding doors that lead to the pool are never locked. Harold admitted that no one even has a key for those doors."

Janet sighed. "So the killer could have simply let himself or herself in through those sliding doors at any time of the day or night."

"Or he or she may already have been inside," Edward pointed out. "John and Sarah are staying in the main house, and all of the staff have rooms here as well."

"And with the horrible weather last night, no one was sitting outside on patios or balconies to notice if someone was heading to the main house late at night," Janet said. "What about a lock on Arthur's bedroom door?"

"There is one, but Mr. Farnsley never used it. Apparently, he used it years ago, when the grandchildren were small and prone to racing around the house and barging in everywhere, but I was told he hadn't bothered to lock his door for years now," Joe told her.

"And where were the nurses?"

"Do you want to see Arthur's suite?" Joe asked.

Janet nodded. "I'm not a trained investigator or anything, though. I'm just being nosy."

Joe chuckled. "I've read the file. I know better than that."

What's in my file? Janet wondered as she got to her feet.

"Let me just make certain that no one will interrupt," Joe said. He sent a text message and then waited for a reply. A moment later, he nodded at Janet and Edward. "We're good."

Edward took Janet's hand as they walked back down the corridor towards the kitchen.

"Is the body still there?" Janet whispered as the thought popped into her head.

"It's being removed now," Joe replied, leaving Janet to worry about her hearing. Clearly her whispers weren't as quiet as she'd believed.

Joe led them into the sitting room. "I thought we could start from here," he said. "We'll retrace Mr. Farnsley's movements from last evening."

Janet nodded. "He was sitting there," she said gesturing towards the appropriate chair. "When he started to get up, Audrey came forwards and helped him."

"And they walked from the chair to the door and then down the corridor," Edward said as they left the room.

"Into this lift," Joe said as he stopped in front of the door to a small lift.

"Where are the stairs?" Janet asked as Joe pressed the button to call the lift.

"At the end of the corridor," he replied, gesturing.

"I'm just going to take a look," Janet said, not entirely certain why it mattered to her.

Edward followed her as she walked past several doors and then stopped.

"That can't be the main staircase for a house this large," Janet said as she looked at the narrow staircase.

"It didn't used to be," Edward replied. "When the house was built, there was a large central staircase, but the house has been altered several times since, and, at some point, the staircase was removed and replaced by the lift. These are the stairs that were originally for the staff, but now anyone who prefers stairs has to use them."

"I'm going to guess that John and Sarah are quite happy using the lift," Janet said. "What about the staff?"

"I believe they typically use the lift, too," Edward replied.

Janet walked up a few steps and then put her hand on the railing. "I don't think anyone has polished the railing recently," she commented as she pulled her hand away.

"I can ask Sammy, or rather, Joe can ask Sammy," Edward said.

Janet nodded. "We need to talk about your connection to the police, too," she whispered as she rejoined him.

"We'll do that," he promised as they walked back to the lift together.

Joe was standing inside it, holding the door open.

"It's not very large," Janet remarked as she entered. "It wouldn't easily fit more than four or five people."

"But it usually has to carry only one or two," Edward replied.

"What about suitcases, or furniture for that matter? How do those get upstairs?" Janet wondered.

"There's a large service lift just outside the staff kitchen," Joe told her. "We can take a look at that later. That's how they'll be taking the body out of the house, although that should already have been accomplished by now."

Janet nodded. When the lift stopped, the doors opened slowly. Janet stepped out of the car and looked up and down the corridor. It was easy enough to guess which was Arthur's bedroom. Police tape had been stretched across the door in a large "X."

"According to Audrey, she and Mr. Farnsley went straight from the lift to his bedroom," Joe said as he led Janet and Edward towards the door.

When they reached it, Joe pulled on a pair of gloves and then detached the tape from one side of the door before pulling out a set of keys.

"We're keeping the door locked," he explained as he

found the right key. "And we're keeping a guard in the room," he added as he pushed the door open.

Janet looked into the room and then hid a smile. A young, uniformed policeman was sitting in a chair near the door. From what Janet could see, he was fast asleep.

"Jacobs?" Joe barked.

The man jumped in his seat and then leaped to his feet. "Sir, Inspector, sir, I was just, that is, I was thinking hard, sir."

"Thinking hard?" Joe echoed. "You were fast asleep."

The young man opened his mouth and then shut it again. "Yes, sir, I was," he admitted after a moment. "I was up late last night, working on my schoolwork. I was fine while I was busy, but once I sat down, I couldn't keep my eyes open."

"I know it's difficult, keeping up with your schoolwork while you're working full-time, but we need a guard in here who is awake and capable," Joe told him. "Go and get yourself some coffee from the office, and then take a brisk walk around the property. Be back in twenty minutes, ready to stay awake for the rest of your shift."

"Yes, sir. I am sorry, sir," the young man said before he disappeared through the door.

"I think it's highly unlikely that anyone got in here in the last few minutes," Joe said. "They've only just removed the body. I'm amazed that Jacobs managed to fall asleep that quickly."

Janet took a look around the small sitting room that they'd entered. The furniture appeared comfortable. The couch and two chairs were all angled to face the small television that was mounted on the wall. There were lamps on two of the tables and a few books on another.

"I'm told that Mr. Farnsley enjoyed spending time in

here, especially in the evening," Joe said. "But last night, after dinner, he went straight to bed."

Janet took a deep breath. "And the bedroom?"

"Is through here," Joe told her. "We've little to no chance of getting any useful evidence from anything in there, but I'm still going to ask you not to touch anything."

Janet nodded and then slid her hands into her pockets, feeling grateful that she always did her best to buy clothing with pockets. The pockets in the trousers she was wearing weren't deep enough to be actually useful for carrying anything, but they were big enough for her hands for the next few minutes.

Joe opened the bedroom door and switched on the light. Janet stood in the doorway and looked at the room.

"I was afraid there would be a lot of blood," she admitted as she stared at the empty bed. She could see some brown stains on the white sheets, but not as much as she'd been expecting.

"I'd rather you didn't walk through the room," Joe said apologetically. "There's an en-suite bathroom through that door." He gestured.

"So where are the nurses' rooms?" Janet asked again.

Joe turned and led her back into the sitting room. There was a door in one wall of the room. "Through here," he explained, opening the door.

Janet followed him into a small corridor. Three doors opened off of it.

"Two bedrooms and a shared bathroom," Joe explained. "The women have been moved into rooms elsewhere in the house, so you can see the rooms if you'd like."

Janet nodded. "If you don't mind."

"Not at all," Joe said. He opened the first door and then stepped back to let Janet look into the room.

"It's very utilitarian, isn't it?" Janet asked as she looked around the small room. The single bed with its bare mattress was pushed against one wall. A cheap wooden wardrobe and a small chest of drawers were the only other furniture in the room.

"The other bedroom is virtually identical," Joe told her.

Janet peeked in just long enough to confirm his opinion. The small bathroom was similarly plain but functional.

"This door opens back into the corridor near the lift," Joe said after he'd shut the door to the bathroom. "We can go back through the sitting room, if you'd rather."

"This is fine," Janet said, frowning. She'd wanted to see the rooms, but now she felt as if she'd wasted Joe's time.

"We allowed both women to take their things," Joe said as the trio made their way back to the lift. "They packed under supervision, but we didn't formally search their rooms or their belongings."

"Where are they now?" Janet asked.

"They've been moved into rooms in the staff wing," Joe said. "There's enough room in that wing for dozens of staff."

"How many guest rooms does the house have?" Janet wondered.

"That depends on how you count guest rooms," Joe replied. "Mr. Farnsley had his room, with the two adjacent rooms for his nurses. Originally, those rooms were used as a nursery and as a bedroom for Mr. John Farnsley's nanny. Mr. John Farnsley and his wife have a similar set of rooms at the other end of this corridor."

He gestured in that direction before pressing the button for the lift.

"Is that all that's on this floor?" Janet asked.

"There are several smaller rooms that are used for storage," Joe told her. "Some of the larger ones could be used as guest rooms, I would imagine, but none of them have en-suite facilities, and I'm fairly certain that Mr. Farnsley's guests would expect to have them."

"I would imagine so," Janet replied.

"The layout of the rooms on the floors above are virtually identical to this one," Joe told her as they walked into the lift. "Each has two suites of rooms with en-suites, sitting rooms, and smaller adjoining bedrooms. There are three additional floors, so a total of six guest suites."

"And yet Mr. Farnsley built cottages for each of his grandchildren," Janet said thoughtfully.

"It gave them more privacy than they would have had staying here," Edward said.

Janet nodded. "I don't understand truly wealthy people."

Joe laughed. "They aren't like you and me," he told Janet with a wink.

The trio walked back to Joe's temporary office.

"Now what?" Janet asked as they all sat back down.

"Now we have to work out who killed Arthur Farnsley," Joe said.

Chapter 12

"That's going to be easier said than done," Joe admitted. "I believe everyone on the island had the means and the opportunity."

"So let's talk about motive," Edward suggested.

"After last night, I would have thought that the family would have wanted him alive for as long as possible," Janet said. "They all wanted a chance to change his mind about the trusts."

"But they were all pretty angry with him," Joe said. "Maybe angry enough to do something stupid."

"I can't see any of them being stupid enough to murder Arthur immediately," Janet said thoughtfully. "As we left last night, they were all talking about ringing their solicitors and fighting Arthur through the courts. They were all upset, but they were all ready to fight for what they felt was theirs."

"Let's talk about each of the couples in turn," Joe said. "And let's start with John and Sarah. They were just down the corridor from Mr. Farnsley, and since they were staying in the house, they probably knew his routine quite well."

"Arthur's new trusts cut his income in half," Edward said.

"And he was understandably upset about that, but as I said earlier, he was getting ready to fight his father through the courts," Janet said.

"I think Sarah may have been more upset," Edward mused. "Not only had their income been cut, but Arthur told everyone about her affair and cast doubts as to the paternity of her son."

Janet nodded. "It was all awful and nasty, especially as it was clear that Arthur was enjoying the revelations. I felt sorrier for Andrew than Sarah at the time, but looking back, it must have been horrible for her."

"So horrible that she'd kill her father-in-law?" Joe asked.

Janet thought for a minute. "From what she said, she wasn't certain who had fathered Andrew. I think, if she'd been sure that John was his father, that she would have been eager to prove Arthur wrong, but under the circumstances, I can see her wanting to get rid of the man, just for being so nasty to her."

"Does that mean she's at the top of your list of suspects?" Edward asked.

"Not at all," Janet said. "I don't have a list yet. I suppose I'd put her just above her husband, though."

"She was upset for both herself and for her son," Joe interjected. "Does that give her an especially strong motive?"

"I would imagine that John was also upset for his son," Janet replied. "Whatever the truth about Sarah's affair, John raised Andrew as his own."

"And whatever happened between him and Sarah all those years ago, they seem happy enough now," Edward added. "Arthur's comments last night must have been difficult for both of them."

Joe made a few notes and then looked up. "What about Phillip and Rachel?" he asked.

"They were the least affected by Arthur's changes to the trust," Edward said. "They lost a quarter of their income, but compared to everyone else, they got off lightly."

"Except they've been trying for a baby for years and haven't managed it," Janet said. "Hearing Arthur demand a great-grandchild must have been difficult for them."

Joe nodded. "Can you see either of them as the killer?"

Janet frowned. "No?" she said, her tone giving away her indecision. "I'd put them under John and Sarah, with Phillip slightly more likely than Rachel."

"I agree," Edward said. "They seem unlikely to me, but until we have more evidence, everyone stays on the list."

"Let's talk about Andrew and Stephanie," Joe said. "He must have been furious when his grandfather suggested that he was the result of an affair."

"It definitely wasn't the first time the idea had been suggested to him," Janet said. "But it was the first time anyone truly seemed to care. As long as John acknowledged him as his son, his biological parent didn't matter."

"Until last night," Joe said.

Janet nodded. "But I can't see that Arthur's death helps in any way. If the trusts have been changed in the manner that Arthur said they have, then Andrew is still going to have to take a DNA test or be disinherited."

"Maybe Stephanie was angry on her husband's behalf, and maybe she doesn't truly understand the trusts," Joe suggested.

Janet laughed. "I'm fairly certain that everyone in the family knows everything there is to know about the trusts," she told him. "At least, the trusts as they were before Arthur started tinkering with them."

"So where are Stephanie and Andrew on your list?" Edward asked.

Janet frowned. "At the bottom, maybe, or maybe equal with Phillip and Rachel. I can't see how Arthur's death helps any of them."

"And that leaves just Brandon and Margaret," Joe said.

"I suppose Brandon is at the top of my list," Janet told him. "He stormed out in the middle of the conversation last night. He may have missed hearing some of the more important details, and his shoes have gone missing, or so he claims."

Joe nodded. "We're still trying to find those shoes," he said. "I have a half-dozen men and women combing the beach as we speak."

"He has a lot to lose if Arthur truly did make the changes to the trusts that he told everyone about last night," Edward said.

"But Margaret could simply divorce him but stay with him," Janet suggested. "They don't have to separate, even if they get legally divorced."

"I can't imagine that Arthur would have approved of that arrangement, but it may work for them now that John will be head of the family," Edward said. "I suspect Arthur would have insisted that Margaret cut all ties with Brandon after their divorce."

"Which gives Brandon and Margaret a motive for the murder," Janet added.

Joe nodded. "He's at the top of my list," he told her. "And her name comes right after his."

"It would be helpful if we could see exactly how the trusts have been rewritten," Janet said. "And that's true for the family as well. Everything that Arthur said last night

The Farnsley Assignment

sounded incredibly complicated, and I wonder how much of it is actually possible – legally, I mean."

"I've spoken to three of Mr. Farnsley's legal team already, and I'm expecting two others to get back to me later today," Joe told her. "I'm hoping to have copies of all of the trust agreements, both old and new, by the end of the day tomorrow. Mr. John Farnsley has also been in touch with his solicitor in London. He's requested the same thing and has promised to share everything he receives with me once it arrives."

"That's all assuming that Arthur was killed because of the trusts, of course," Janet said.

"Are you suggesting that someone had some other motive?" Joe asked.

Janet shrugged. "It's possible. We haven't talked about the staff yet."

Joe looked as if he wanted to argue, but after a moment, he sat back in his seat and smiled at Janet. "By all means, talk about the staff," he said.

"Harold had been working for Mr. Farnsley for a number of years," Janet said. "I hope he was being well paid for his time."

"He was," Edward told her. "He was paid a generous salary that came straight out of one of the trusts. It included an annual cost of living rise and bonuses based on years of service."

"But did he enjoy his work? How well did he get along with Mr. Farnsley?" Janet asked.

"Obviously, we'll be investigating their relationship, but thus far I've seen nothing that raises any red flags," Joe told her.

"What about Stuart, the chef?" Janet asked. "He travelled with Mr. Farnsley, too, didn't he?"

"He travelled between New York and Farntopia with

Arthur, but Arthur had another chef that he used when he was in London," Edward told her.

"How long had Stuart been working for Arthur?" Janet asked. That information had been in the file she'd been given before they'd arrived, but she'd forgotten a lot of what she'd read.

"About ten years," Edward told her. "When Arthur was in London, Stuart was paid a retainer and allowed to remain in his suite of rooms in Arthur's New York home. Arthur's chef in London works on a similar arrangement."

"So half of the year he's paid for not working?" Janet asked.

"Something like that," Edward replied.

"I can't imagine him wanting to do anything to harm Arthur," Janet said.

"Unless Arthur was thinking about getting rid of him," Joe suggested. "Perhaps he thinks that Mr. John Farnsley is more likely to keep him on."

Janet shrugged. "I know people get murdered over all manner of little things, but killing someone to keep a job, even a really good job, seems extreme."

"Which puts Stuart near the bottom of my list," Edward told her. "He and Harold are both at the very bottom, actually, unless we later discover something that gives one of them a stronger motive."

"What about Sammy?" Janet asked.

"He lives here full-time," Joe told her. "We keep an eye on him."

"Oh?" Janet replied.

"He got into quite a bit of trouble when he was younger," Joe explained. "But he's cleaned up his act a lot over the last few years. Mr. Farnsley pays him well, and as far as I know, he works hard and does a good job on Farntopia."

"No hint that Arthur might have been thinking about getting rid of him?" Edward asked.

"Not that I've heard, but I don't hear everything. I'll ask Harold. He would know if Mr. Farnsley was considering making any changes on the island," Joe replied.

"What about the nurses?" Janet asked.

"What about them? They both came from the same UK agency. They've both worked for Mr. Farnsley for over a year. As far as I know, he was happy with both of them and their work," Joe told her.

Janet frowned. "They told me that Arthur suffered from insomnia, but Dawn said he never rang for her last night."

"Maybe, having upset everyone in the house, he slept well for a change," Edward suggested.

"What a horrible thought," Janet replied.

"Do you suspect one of them?" Joe asked.

"I wouldn't say that," Janet replied thoughtfully. "I can't imagine a motive for either of them."

"Especially since they'll now both be out of a job," Edward said. "The others can all hope that John will keep them on, but he and Sarah have no need for nurses. Both Dawn and Audrey will have to return to England and try to find new assignments."

"Maybe one of them was tired of working for Arthur and decided to get rid of him," Janet suggested.

"Surely quitting is a good deal easier," Joe replied with a small chuckle.

"I don't suppose either of them has a history of leaving behind patients who'd passed away under mysterious circumstances," Janet said.

Edward frowned. "You really didn't care for them, then."

"There was something odd about both of them," Janet

said. "Maybe it's still bothering me that they look so much alike. They aren't related in any way, are they?"

"I don't believe so," Joe said. "But we can check."

"You should," Edward told him. "Janet has great instincts."

She blushed. "I've also been known to be wrong. Don't waste too much time or energy on Dawn and Audrey."

Joe nodded. "They had the best access to Mr. Farnsley. We were going to take a close look at them, regardless."

"Where are they on your list, then?" Edward asked Janet.

"I've no idea," she said after a minute. "Something is bothering me about both of them, but that may just be me. I suppose I'd put them under Brandon and Margaret, as they may actually have had something to gain from Arthur's death. Assuming Arthur was telling the truth about the trusts, everyone else seems to have had reasons to want him alive."

"We could speculate all day about the wording in the trusts and how it might be affected by Arthur's death, but for now I think we need to let Joe get on with his investigation," Edward said, getting to his feet. "And we need to get on with pretending to be on holiday."

"And I have to start being nasty and demanding again," Janet said with a tired sigh.

"You should be enjoying it," Joe suggested. "I'd love a chance to be rich and obnoxious for a few days."

"It simply isn't in my nature," Janet replied. "Maybe that's what's bothering me about the nurses, actually. I wanted to hear more of their stories and find out about them as people, but I had to pretend I wasn't interested."

"Let's go and see whom we can find for a chat," Edward suggested as Janet stood up. "It would be nice if we could talk to everyone, at least briefly."

"That sounds incredibly ambitious," Joe said.

"Ambitious, but useful," Edward replied. "But first I need to have a private chat with my wife. She was previously unaware of some of the more interesting parts of my past." He looked at Joe. "My past as Edward Thomas-Blanchard, that is. Janet knows everything there is to know about Edward Bennett."

Not hardly, Janet thought as she let Edward lead her out of the room. While Edward had shared a handful of stories about his years working for the agency with her, she knew that they'd been carefully edited stories that covered no more than a handful of the dozens of assignments that he'd undertaken over the years.

They walked together back to their cottage. Once they were inside, Edward pulled her into a kiss.

"I should have done that back in Joe's office," he said when he lifted his head. "It's been a long day," he added as they sat down together on the nearest couch.

"And it isn't even dinner time yet," Janet pointed out.

"We'll be having dinner with the family at six. Joe has already discussed it with Harold. We'll be joined by the staff, aside from Stuart and Harold, who will be preparing the meal and serving it, respectively."

"So Sammy and the nurses will be joining us."

"Yes, something that Janet Smythson Thomas-Blanchard might find objectionable."

"But she may be too fed up with the entire situation to complain. I believe she really just wants off the island, as beautiful as it is. She may be worried about her personal safety. There is a murderer on the island, after all."

"Harold and Joe have arranged for a team of security guards to be flown out to the island. They should be here by the time we finish with dinner. A guard is going to be assigned to each of the cottages with a further two to be stationed in the house. Joe wants to make certain that everyone feels safe and that the murderer gets nervous."

Janet raised an eyebrow. "Who is paying for all of this?"

"Joe made the arrangements through Mr. Jones. I don't think John needs to worry about the expense."

"Surely we're unnecessary if there are going to be that many security people around."

"We're not here to protect anyone or anything," Edward told her.

"So why are we here?"

"I wish I knew."

Janet sighed. "You were going to tell me about your criminal past."

Edward looked shocked. "How dare you imply that I was ever a criminal," he said teasingly. "I'm afraid my modified life history isn't that interesting, but Mr. Jones needed to come up with something that would make sense under the circumstances."

"So what do I need to know?"

"I'm almost nervous to tell you. It had to be something that Edward Thomas-Blanchard would never have told Janet Smythson, but still nothing criminal."

Janet thought for a moment. "It will be something from long before we met and presumably long before you became a wealthy businessman."

"My father was a policeman," Edward told her.

"Your father was a policeman? How common," Janet said with a wink.

"He and my mother divorced when I was only five and Mother remarried within a year. Wilfred Thomas-Blanchard, my stepfather, adopted me, but my biological father agreed to allow it only if he was still given some visitation rights. So I spent a few weeks each summer with my biological father, who did his best to encourage me to follow in his footsteps."

"As a policeman?" Janet asked incredulously.

Edward chuckled. "It's a ridiculous notion, of course, but my father didn't see it that way. He often told me that my mother was probably going to throw me out once I turned eighteen, and that I'd have to find a way to survive on my own."

"What a horrible thing to say to a child." Janet was angry on behalf of the child Edward had never actually been.

"Yes, well, I do believe that he meant well, but he was wrong, of course. Wilfred and my mother never managed to have any additional children. When Wilfred died, he left everything to my mother. She passed away a year later, leaving everything to me."

"Which made you a very wealthy young man," Janet suggested.

Edward nodded. "But one who hadn't forgotten where he'd come from. I bought my biological father a house and a car and did my best to persuade him to retire. He refused, as he felt he still had a lot of good to do in the world. We used to take a fortnight's holiday together every summer, wherever he wanted to go. Over the years, I met several of his work colleagues, and when my father passed away, I met quite a few more at his funeral. Since then, I've kept in touch with one or two of the men who were both colleagues and friends, and when I found the body this morning, I rang one of them. Obviously, he's back in the UK and couldn't help directly, but he knew exactly whom to contact to get the investigation started."

"It's all a bit convoluted."

"It is, but it was the best that Mr. Jones could do on short notice. Remember that I was supposed to have been at school with John. That made it impossible for me to have had any old school friends who were now with the police. The men who went to the boarding school where John went do not join the police after university."

Janet sighed. "Maybe the world would be a better place if they did."

Edward shrugged. "Some of them join the agency."

"And one of them is now Smith?" Janet guessed.

"Let's not go there."

"So what do we do now?"

"Now, we have to start talking to everyone so that we can help Joe find the killer. Before we do that, though, is there anything you didn't tell him that I need to know?"

Janet blinked at him. "Are you suggesting that I withheld information from a police officer?"

"What was I thinking?" Edward asked. "Janet Markham Bennett, I love you."

He pulled her close and then kissed her.

"Is there anything you need to tell me?" she asked. "I didn't hear your interview with Joe."

"I should tell you what happened this morning, actually, but that won't take long."

He settled back in his seat and pulled her closer.

"Are you okay?" she asked.

"Finding murder victims is always awful," he replied. "I thought Arthur was rather horrible last night, but no one deserves to be killed while sleeping."

Janet shuddered. "You don't have to tell me anything."

"I do, though. You need to know everything I told Joe if we're going to help solve the case."

"I hope we can help, anyway."

Edward nodded. "When I got to the house, Harold let me in and told me that Arthur was still sleeping. We chatted for a few minutes, and then I insisted that I be allowed to speak to Arthur. I got the impression that Harold was rather happy to allow me to wake the man, but I'm not certain why."

"Something to ask Harold, then," Janet suggested.

"Perhaps, but I may want to think about it for a while before I ask. Anyway, I persuaded Harold to take me to Arthur's suite. The door wasn't locked. Harold suggested that I knock and then wait in the sitting room until Arthur could join me there. He seemed to be anticipating an ugly scene, really, by that point."

"How nice."

Edward shrugged. "I knocked and then walked into the sitting room, calling Arthur's name. When no one replied, I knocked on the bedroom door. Again no one replied, but I told Harold that I thought I'd heard someone say something. When I opened the bedroom door, it was clear that Arthur was dead."

Janet squeezed him tightly. "I'm sorry," she said softly. "That must have been horrible for you."

"Thank you," he replied as a single tear slid down his cheek. He wiped it away and stared at her. "I've been doing this for a long time, and this is the first time anyone has ever sympathised with me over what I've found. I'm not crying over Arthur's death. I'm just a bit overcome because someone actually cares how I feel."

Janet felt her own eyes fill with tears. "You have me now and forever," she told him. "Even if I'm going to pretend to be a demanding and spoiled cow for the rest of this assignment."

Edward was still chuckling as they got up to get ready to go.

Chapter 13

"Should I dress for dinner, or for a stroll around the island?" Janet asked as she opened the wardrobe.

"Dress for dinner, but wear comfortable shoes," he suggested.

Janet frowned. "I have plenty of comfortable shoes, but I don't know that Janet Smythson would wear them."

"I doubt anyone will be paying any attention to your shoes tonight. It's been a long and difficult day for everyone."

Janet changed into a summery dress, one that Edward had bought for her in London. She knew it had been expensive, because the shop hadn't had any price tags on anything that was on display. Edward had insisted that she needed a few special outfits in her wardrobe just in case they were ever sent on a last-minute assignment. Now she was glad she hadn't argued with him.

"Do these shoes look okay?" she asked as she slid on a pair of sandals. They were also new and had cost more than Janet typically spent on footwear, but she was well aware that they hadn't actually been all that expensive, at least not by Farnsley family standards.

"You look lovely," Edward told her.

"And you look very handsome," she replied, giving him a quick kiss.

Edward's clothes always looked expensive, and tonight was no exception. He slid his wallet into his pocket and then offered Janet his arm.

"Whom do we want to find first?" she asked as they walked down the stairs together.

"I don't really mind. I just hope we get to speak to everyone, although we should see them all at dinner, if not before."

They walked outside and Janet frowned. "It's very hot out here."

"It is. Maybe it would be cooler by the water."

"Or maybe we should go back inside our air-conditioned cottage for now. Surely someone from the main cottage can come and collect us in the golf cart in time for dinner."

Edward sighed. "I thought we were going to take a walk on the beach."

"And I thought you were the son of a successful businessman," she snapped before she turned and strode down the beach towards the water.

Within seconds, she'd reached Rachel, who had been obviously listening to the entire exchange.

"Good evening," Janet said.

"Good evening," Rachel replied. "How are you tonight?"

Janet sighed deeply. "Feeling rather desperate to get off this island," she said. "I've been told that is impossible at the moment, though."

Rachel nodded. "We're eager to leave as well. Phillip

wants to talk to his solicitors about the changes to the trusts, and I'm ready to start trying for a baby again. At least, I think I am."

Janet took a slow deep breath to stop herself from being sympathetic. "Perhaps, now that Arthur is gone, the trusts will go back to the way they were before he started making changes."

"I think we're all hoping for that, but he was adamant last night that the changes were done and that we couldn't do anything about it."

"But now that he's gone, surely John will be in charge of the trusts. Whatever loophole Arthur was able to exploit, surely John can use the same one to change everything back."

"Except knowing John, he'll change everything in a totally different way," Rachel said, a touch of bitterness in her tone. "Oh, I'm sure he'll be less awful than Arthur was, but he'll also do what he can to enrich himself at everyone else's expense."

"What a shame. My husband, my first husband, left me everything, which upset my children a bit. They seemed to think that they should be entitled to something, but obviously St. John didn't see it that way. They will be disappointed when I die, as I've left nearly everything to charity, but they won't discover that until I'm no longer here to enjoy their reactions."

Rachel stared at her for a moment. "Do you have grandchildren?"

Janet frowned. "I suppose I might, but I don't believe so. No, of course not. If one of the children had managed to procreate, he or she would have informed me, no doubt expecting a generous gift in exchange for the news."

"I should go," Rachel said after an awkward moment.

"We're all supposed to have dinner at the main house tonight in an hour or so."

Janet nodded. "I was informed. I suggested to Edward that we decline under the circumstances, but as neither of us cooks, we have little choice."

"I'll see you later, then," Rachel said before she turned and walked rapidly towards her cottage.

"You were horrible," Edward said as he walked up behind her.

Janet grinned. "I may have been a little bit too nasty about my children. I'm sure Ermine and Wolf are wonderful, really."

"Maybe we should go and visit them after we leave here."

"You say that as if you expect us to be leaving together," Janet said as she spotted someone walking towards them.

"Of course I expect us to be together," Edward replied. "You're my wife, and I love you."

Janet shrugged. "You say that, but you lied to me."

"I didn't lie. I simply didn't tell you everything."

"The identity of your biological father is a pretty important thing to have left out," Janet snapped. She turned to Stephanie. "Don't you agree?" she demanded.

"I may be the wrong person to ask, as it seems likely that my husband neglected to mention the true identity of his father," Stephanie replied flatly.

"Except he didn't know that until yesterday," Janet replied. "My husband, on the other hand, knew perfectly well that his father was, well, not the man who raised him."

Stephanie shrugged. "I don't see why it matters. Anyone can do what's needed to make a baby. Parenting a child is much more difficult. My own parents weren't particularly interested in their children. One of the reasons that I fell in love with Andrew was because of how close he was to his parents. They have a family island," she said waving at the sea and the sand.

"It's very nice," Janet said unenthusiastically.

"I just hope that John can stop whatever Arthur did," Stephanie said.

"Of course, because Andrew's inheritance is at stake," Janet suggested.

"And because Andrew's relationship with his entire family is at stake," Stephanie replied. "If he isn't John's biological child, that will change everything. His sister has already said a few horrible things to him, and that husband of hers is even worse. I'm not certain that refusing to take a DNA test is going to be possible now, though. Everyone wants to know the truth. Everyone but Andrew, anyway."

"Including you?" Janet had to ask.

"I just want all of the awfulness to stop, and I can't see that happening if Andrew won't take the test," she said.

"Even if Arthur never actually changed the trusts?" Edward asked.

"This isn't about money anymore. Arthur's words last night changed everything. He's instilled doubts in everyone's mind, and there's only going to be one way to get rid of those doubts. I just have to convince Andrew of that."

"Good luck," Janet told her.

"Thank you." She stopped and then turned and looked at Edward. "I wanted to ask you," she began.

"Yes?" he said.

"I don't know anything about your connection to the police, but I thought maybe you would tell me how these sorts of investigations work. I suppose I'm mostly curious about how long we'll have to stay on the island," she replied.

Edward shook his head. "I'm afraid I have no idea how

long the investigation will take. Things are done very differently here from how they're done in London. Inspector Price has said that we'll all be asked to remain here until the initial investigation is complete. I'm hoping that won't take more than a few days."

"Only a few days," Stephanie repeated. "I'm going to hold on to that and repeat it as a mantra when it all gets overwhelming. I hope you're right."

"We'll see you at dinner shortly," Janet said as the woman began to walk away.

Stephanie turned back towards her and frowned. "We were talking about skipping dinner. It's going to be awkward and awful, and I swear if Margaret or Brandon say anything at all to Andrew, I'll punch them both."

"Maybe it would be best if you didn't come to dinner," Janet said.

"But we do need to eat," Stephanie replied. "I'm a terrible cook, and Andrew can make only two things, and we don't have the ingredients for either."

"That's two more than I can make," Janet told her.

"I suppose I'll see you at dinner, then," Stephanie said before she turned around again and headed up the beach.

"Interesting," Janet murmured.

"Let's walk a bit further," Edward suggested. "We can pretend to argue more about my past, or we can pretend to be ignoring one another while walking together."

"Look at this amazing scenery. How can anyone be angry while surrounded by all of this amazing scenery?"

Edward took her hand and they continued along the beach, past the last of the guest cottages. From there, a path led up to the road that ran behind the cottages and led to the main house.

"Let's see where the road goes," Edward suggested. He looked at his watch. "Or let's see how far we can get in ten minutes, at least. Then we'll have to turn around or else we'll be late for dinner."

They walked a short distance before they heard the sound of a motor.

"Here comes the golf cart," Edward said.

Janet looked further down the road and saw the small cart rushing towards them. She and Edward stepped off the road and into the sand as the cart got closer. The two nurses were both wearing shorts, T-shirts, and oversized sunglasses. With their hair in matching ponytails, Janet was struck again by how much they looked alike.

"Hello," Audrey called from behind the steering wheel. "We thought we were going to be late for dinner, but if you're out here, we must be okay."

"We thought it might be nice to take a stroll before dinner," Edward told her.

"It's a lovely evening for walking," Dawn said from the cart's passenger seat. "We wanted to go down to the waterfall, so we took the golf cart."

"With Harold's permission," Audrey added quickly.

Dawn laughed. "Yes, of course, with Harold's permission. No one seems to know what to do with us now that we no longer have a patient to look after. I dare say we don't know what to do with ourselves, either. I took a nap this afternoon, but when I woke up, I didn't have any other ideas of things to do."

"So I suggested that we could drive down to the waterfall," Audrey took up the story. "We used to take Mr. Farnsley down there once in a while, the last time we were here. He hadn't been up to it this time."

"Is it far?" Janet asked.

"Not terribly, but you should probably take a cart, rather than try to walk. And stay out of the water, as it is considerably deeper than it looks, and there are strong currents there," Dawn told her.

"There are strong currents all around the island, or so Mr. Farnsley told me," Audrey said. "He said it was okay to splash in the water on the beach, but that it wasn't safe to try to swim anywhere around the island."

"That's good to know," Janet said. "Not that I was planning to do any swimming."

"There's a pool for that," Dawn told her. "I may spend the entire day at the pool tomorrow, actually. No one else ever uses it."

"We used to take Mr. Farnsley in the pool once in a while," Audrey reminded her.

"Okay, yes, but only because we suggested it, and we always had it all to ourselves when we did," Dawn replied.

Janet looked down the road and then glanced at her watch. "Maybe we should walk down to the waterfall after dinner."

"Let's see how much wine I have with dinner," Edward replied with a wink.

"You do drink too much wine," Janet replied with a frown. "But I want to see the waterfall."

"We'll still be here tomorrow, and I dare say the waterfall will, too."

Janet frowned and then nodded as Edward gave her a peculiar look. "Or maybe I'll drink too much wine, and then you can look after me after dinner," she said. "It feels as if it's the perfect night for too much wine."

"I'll drink to that," Dawn said firmly.

"Me, too," Audrey added.

"Now, do you two want a ride to the main house?" Dawn asked.

Janet looked at Edward. "That would be wonderful," Janet said as she climbed into the back of the golf cart.

"Edward is far more fond of walking than I am. I suppose that comes from his unfortunate childhood. My husband, St. John, he didn't walk until he was nearly two. His nannies always carried him everywhere, and, apparently, it never occurred to him to actually make the effort to walk himself. Of course, once he began walking, he also began running, and he was very nearly an Olympic-quality sprinter in his university days. He preferred to devote his time to his studies, rather than running. Otherwise, he might have been a contender on the international stage."

"Are either of your children good runners?" Edward asked with a sly grin.

Janet stared at him for a moment. "No," she said icily.

"What did you tell me your daughter is called?" Dawn asked as Audrey pulled the cart up behind the house.

"Ermine," Janet replied. "Like the fur, which is a particular favourite of mine. After Ermine was born, St. John gave me a full-length ermine coat."

"What did you get when you had Wolf?" Edward asked.

Janet turned a burst of laughter into a cough. "Diamonds," she replied lightly, once she'd regained control.

"Diamonds?" Dawn echoed as they all climbed out of the cart.

"Five-carat earrings, ten carats in total," Janet told her. "Sadly, they have to be kept in a safe in my London home, and I can wear them only very occasionally, but they are stunning."

"I'd be happy with just one tiny diamond," Dawn said. "I'm still hoping to find a man one day who wants to buy me a ring. My mother reckons I'm too old, but I haven't given up yet."

"You're never too old to find love," Janet said firmly.

"But while you're waiting for a man, why don't you buy yourself a diamond or two?"

Dawn looked at her for a moment and then laughed. "I could, you know. I could buy myself a wonderful, sparkly diamond ring that would make me smile every time I wore it."

"Jewellery isn't practical when you're working," Audrey remarked.

"No, but I don't work all the time," Dawn replied. "I'm planning to take at least a few weeks off once I get back to the UK. Maybe I'll spend some of my holiday shopping for jewellery."

"I hope you do," Janet told her.

Edward took her hand and gave it a gentle squeeze. Janet sighed. She knew she was being too nice, but surely sometimes even Janet Smythson had a heart.

"I shall be going back to work immediately," Audrey said as they began to walk towards the house.

"You said before that you've been saving your money," Janet remarked. "Are you saving for something special?"

"I want…" Audrey began. Then she shook her head and shrugged. "Saving money just seems smart. My mother spent every penny that passed through her hands, often on foolish or frivolous things. I suppose that's made me extra cautious."

Harold was standing in the doorway when they reached the house.

"I was afraid I was going to have to tell Stuart to delay dinner," he said disapprovingly. "I never would have let you take the cart out if I'd known you were going to be gone this long."

Audrey flushed as Dawn replied.

"We were on our way back when we nearly ran down Mr. and Mrs. Thomas-Blanchard," she said. "They asked us where the road went, so we told them all about the waterfall, and then we offered them a ride back here."

"Dinner will be served in six minutes," Harold replied.

"We'd better go and get changed," Dawn said. She and Audrey rushed away together, hurrying towards the lift.

"I am sorry," Harold said to Janet and Edward. "I should not have talked to the other staff in that way in front of you."

Janet shrugged. "I would hate to think that dinner will be late because of them. I'm starving. Lunch seems to have been both inadequate and a very long time ago."

"Dinner will be served on time. If anyone is late, he or she will be given a plate in the kitchen," Harold replied.

"I assume that means that everyone else is already here," Edward said.

Harold frowned. "Actually, you're the first to arrive, but Sammy is going to go out with the golf cart to find everyone. He was simply waiting until Ms. Becker and Ms. Fowler returned."

"Is there only one golf cart on the island?" Janet asked.

"We have others, but we don't put petrol in them unless they're likely to be used. As we were expecting to be here for only the weekend, it seemed unlikely that we would need more than the one that we filled with petrol on arrival," Harold explained.

"How are you?" Janet asked. As soon as the words were out of her mouth, she regretted them. While Janet Markham Bennett was genuinely concerned about the man who'd been working for Arthur for several years and might have felt as if he'd lost a friend, Janet Smythson should not have cared in the slightest.

Harold shrugged. "I've been better. Mr. Farnsley could be difficult, but I believe he was a good person, and he treated me well. It's going to be a challenge to find a new situation that I will enjoy as much as I've enjoyed working for Mr. Farnsley."

"Difficult how?" Edward asked.

"He enjoyed winding people up," Harold explained. "For example, he'd tell me that we were expecting a dozen guest for dinner just a few hours before a meal was due to be served and then sit back and watch as I'd scramble to put together a menu and help the chef prepare everything. When six o'clock came, he'd laugh and then invite all of the staff to join him for the meal."

"You heard what he told his family last night," Edward said. "Do you think he was simply winding everyone up, or do you think that he genuinely made changes to the trusts?"

Harold sighed. "I wish I knew. I do know that he spent a lot of time with all of his solicitors over the past few months, but he always sent me away whenever they arrived."

"Was that typical?" Edward asked.

"Not at all. I usually accompanied him everywhere that he went, from doctors' appointments to meetings with his bank manager to dinner parties with friends."

"But he didn't include you in the meetings with his solicitors," Janet said thoughtfully.

The door suddenly opened behind them, and all the Farnsley grandchildren and their spouses walked into the house together.

Harold snapped to attention and then looked at the grandfather clock nearby. "Dinner will be served in one minute," he said before he turned on his heel and strode out of the room.

Chapter 14

"That doesn't give us much time for a drink before dinner," Margaret complained. "I think I can just about manage to get through a glass of wine in a minute, though."

She quickly walked into the house, heading for the sitting room. The others followed at a more leisurely pace. Sammy was behind the bar when they all arrived. He was pouring wine into glasses and setting them on the bar.

Margaret grabbed a glass with each hand and quickly downed half the contents of one of the glasses.

"Slow down," John told her as he and Sarah entered the room. "The police are going to be joining us at dinner."

"Are they?" Margaret asked. "Why should I care?"

"Because you don't want to say anything that might incriminate you?" Rachel suggested.

Margaret stared at her with narrowed eyes. "What is that supposed to mean?" she demanded.

"Nothing," Phillip said firmly. "Have some wine," he told Rachel.

She reached for a glass and then shook her head. "I'd rather not."

"Because now that Grandfather has given you an incentive, you're suddenly eager for a baby," Margaret suggested as she finished her first glass of wine. "Brandon and I are going to start trying as soon as I can get off my birth control. I rang my doctor last night, and I have an appointment to see him the minute I get home."

"Except we've no idea when we're going to get off this island," Stephanie said.

Margaret shrugged. "My doctor will see me whenever I get back to London. And then I can get started on a baby."

"Maybe you should wait until we've heard from the solicitors," Andrew suggested. "You'll want to be certain that you're doing everything according to the exact terms of the trust."

"Maybe, or maybe you're just saying that to encourage me to wait longer and, in the meantime, you and Stephanie are going to do everything you can to get pregnant," Margaret said.

Andrew shrugged. "Stephanie and I aren't planning on trying for a baby until everything to do with the trusts is cleared up. If I am going to lose my income, having a baby would be a very irresponsible thing to do."

"So it's just you and me," Margaret said to Rachel. "I'd wish you luck, but I really hope you don't manage to get pregnant until after I'm well on my way."

"Shouldn't you be more worried about your marriage than making a baby right now?" Rachel asked angrily.

Margaret shrugged. "Brandon and I are very happy together, aren't we?" she replied, looking at Brandon.

"Yes, of course," he replied.

Since he'd entered the room, he'd steadily worked his way through two glasses of wine, outdrinking the others, even his wife. Now he picked up a third glass and took a sip.

"Good evening," Joe Price said as he walked into the room. "I hope you don't mind me joining you for dinner."

"Of course not," John said stiffly.

Joe grinned at him. "I'm waiting for your father's solicitor to ring me back – the one in London who, I'm told, was charged with coordinating the efforts of the various lawyers, solicitors, and whatnot who worked for your father."

John nodded. "My father used their services for decades. My solicitor is also a part of the same firm."

"We may have answers about the trusts by the time we finish dinner," Joe said.

"That would be good news for everyone," John replied.

"We're not late," Dawn said as she and Audrey rushed into the room. Both women had changed into sleeveless dresses, worn with low heels. They walked a few feet into the room and then stopped. They exchanged glances and then both women took a step backwards.

"Have a drink," John suggested. "We appreciate how hard you worked on behalf of my father. For the remaining days on the island, you're my guests."

Audrey flushed and began to shake her head as Dawn smiled broadly.

"Wow, that's really nice of you," she said as she walked to the bar and picked up a glass of wine. "And this is delicious," she added after a sip.

"I believe everyone is here now," John said to Sammy.

He nodded. "I'll just let Harold know that you're ready."

"I thought Sammy was joining us at dinner," Janet whispered to Edward.

He shrugged. "Perhaps Harold decided to put him to work instead."

Janet watched as Sammy pulled out his mobile and sent a quick text message. Harold walked into the room a moment later.

"Dinner is served," he announced.

Sammy picked up one of the untouched wine glasses in front of him and took a sip as everyone began to leave the room. Janet found herself lingering, wanting to keep an eye on Sammy, but not sure why.

"Shall we?" Edward asked.

Janet reached down to pick up her handbag that she'd set on the table next to her while everyone had been drinking. As she did so, she accidentally tipped it upside down and a half-dozen things spilled out onto the floor.

"And I haven't even been drinking," Janet said with a sigh as she got down on her hands and knees to collect everything. When she got back up, only Edward and Joe remained in the room, aside from Sammy, who was still behind the bar, sipping his wine and watching her with an amused look on his face.

Janet checked that her bag was tightly closed, and then she took Edward's arm and left the room, her head held high. When they reached the dining room, they found everyone sitting in the same seats as they had the previous evening. Arthur's chair had been left empty. As Janet sat down next to Stephanie, Edward took the seat on her other side. The two nurses sat together, opposite Janet and Edward.

As Janet went to hang her handbag off the back of the chair, she had a sudden thought. "My mobile isn't here," she told Edward. "I must have missed it when everything spilled. I'll be right back."

It only took her a moment to reach the sitting room.

"…coming on Tuesday. Everyone needs to be gone by then," Sammy was saying.

"They'll be gone," Joe assured him. "Even your mate Brandon."

"He isn't my mate, but he's very useful. He's just the right mix of stupidity and overconfidence."

"And won't Margaret be surprised when her husband gets himself arrested?" Joe laughed.

"She shouldn't be. She ought to know what sort of man she married."

"But she doesn't."

"Not yet, anyway."

"Taking his shoes was one of your better ideas. They'll come in handy when we need to frame him for something in the future. Now, though, I'd better get in there," Joe said. "Where are you going to be?"

"I was supposed to join you all for dinner, but I'd rather not. Maybe I'll take a walk around the island and just make certain that everything is as it should be."

"That would probably be smart."

Janet quickly took a few steps backwards and then began to mutter to herself.

"…on the walk around the island, so it simply must be here somewhere," she was saying as she dug around in her handbag. She kept her eyes on the bag's interior and let herself walk directly into Joe, who was studying his mobile phone as he walked towards her.

"Ouch," she said distinctly as they collided in the doorway to the sitting room.

"I am sorry," he said quickly. "I wasn't watching where I was going. I just got an important text."

"And I was looking in my bag for my phone," she replied. "I can't find it anywhere. I'm hoping it dropped out when I spilled my bag earlier."

The Farnsley Assignment

She walked across the room to where she'd been standing earlier and then carefully got down on her hands and knees. Aware that both Joe and Sammy were watching her closely, she put her bag down and then leaned down to look under the nearest chair.

"Aha!" she announced before reaching under the chair. The phone was just out of her reach. Sighing, she lay down on the carpet and stretched her arm out under the chair. "Got it," she said happily as she pulled the phone out from where she'd kicked it earlier. "And it's covered with dust. Someone needs to learn how to clean properly."

"It's the sand," Sammy told her. "It gets everywhere."

"Yes, well, it's unacceptable," Janet told him as she brushed off her phone and then slipped it into her bag. She rubbed her hands together and then made a face. "I need to wash my hands," she said.

"There's a loo right outside the door," Sammy told her.

"I can show you," Joe offered.

Janet smiled gratefully at him and then let him lead her to the small loo. She sent a text message and then washed her hands. After taking a deep breath, she opened the door. As she'd expected, Joe was waiting for her right outside.

"Next time, I'll make Edward get on the floor to find my phone," she told him. "I probably should have asked Sammy to do it, actually."

"That would have been more in keeping with your character," Joe agreed. "Although I'll warn you against trusting Sammy."

"Oh?" Janet replied. "I thought you said that he'd cleaned up his act and was working hard here."

Joe shrugged. "That's what I was told, but I'm starting to question my sources."

Janet gasped. "Do you think he killed Arthur?" she asked, wide-eyed.

"That's one possibility."

"Janet? Joe? Is everything okay?" Edward asked as he approached them.

"I found my phone, but it was covered in dust or sand or something," Janet explained. "Joe was kind enough to show me to the nearest loo so I could wash my hands."

"Stuart is ready to serve," Edward told them.

"And I'm starving," Joe said. "After you," he added, gesturing for Janet to go first.

Janet smiled. "Thank you," she said as she turned and walked down the corridor.

Joe said something to Edward, and then the two men stopped. Janet thought about waiting for them, but decided against it. Instead, she walked back into the dining room and smiled at everyone.

"I found my mobile, but it was under a chair, and I had a terrible time retrieving it," she told them.

"You should have told me," Harold said. "I would have taken care of it."

"It's fine," Janet replied as she slid back into her seat.

Edward and Joe arrived less than a minute later. As Edward took his seat, Joe sat down on Edward's other side.

"We're starting tonight with onion soup," Harold announced. He left the room and then returned with a tray full of soup bowls. After everyone had been served, the room fell into an uneasy silence as people began to eat.

"This is delicious," Joe said after his first bite. "But I rarely eat fancy food."

"That makes two of us," Dawn told him, giving him a warm smile.

Joe grinned at her. "There are some nice restaurants in Nassau."

"Are there?" Dawn replied.

"Maybe we could check one out together," Joe suggested. "Once everyone is allowed to leave the island."

"And once she's no longer a suspect in a murder investigation," John suggested.

Dawn blushed and looked down at her soup bowl.

Joe just chuckled. "Yes, of course, that, but we should have the investigation wrapped up fairly quickly."

"Oh?" John replied.

"I'm afraid I can't say anything more than that," Joe said. "At the moment, I'm almost more interested in what the solicitor is going to say."

"We're all eager to hear that," Margaret said as she reached for her wine glass.

"Maybe you should stay sober, then, or fairly sober, anyway," Andrew suggested.

Margaret made a face at him. "Weekends on Farntopia are always best endured through a mild alcoholic blur."

Phillip laughed. "She isn't wrong," he said, reaching for his wine glass.

"Grandfather hated when we drank too much," Andrew said. "I was the only one who was dumb enough to care what Grandfather thought."

"More fool you, because he wasn't even your grandfather," Margaret laughed.

"He may have been," Sarah said sharply. "I had one minor indiscretion in all of my years of marriage. John has forgiven me. It shouldn't matter to anyone else."

"Only one indiscretion?" Brandon asked as Harold began to clear away the empty soup bowls.

Sarah's cheeks flooded with colour. "I can't see why my private life is any of your concern," she replied.

"So that's a no, then," Margaret said with a laugh.

"Be careful, or Father might start questioning your

paternity," Stephanie warned her. "Then you could find yourself without an income, too."

"My father would never do that to me," Margaret said confidently.

"I hope you're certain about that," Brandon said.

"What does that mean?" Margaret demanded.

"Nothing," Brandon muttered.

"I hope you aren't suggesting that you'd leave me if I got cut off," Margaret said angrily.

He shrugged. "Just last night – was it only last night? Just last night, you were considering divorcing me because you didn't think our marriage was going to last forever."

"So? I wasn't planning on leaving you, not really. I was just going to get a divorce to keep Grandfather happy," Margaret told him.

"Whatever," he said.

"Beef in brandy sauce with duchess potatoes and roasted vegetables," Harold announced from the doorway. He carried in a tray and then served half the table. He was back a minute later with the rest of the plates. Janet couldn't help but smile as he put the plate in front of her. Everything looked wonderful.

"What does anyone think of England's chances at the cricket?" Edward asked as people began to eat.

Janet let the conversation wash over her as she ate. She knew very little about cricket generally and even less about England's current team. A few of the names that John and Edward mentioned sounded familiar to her, but either of them could have added in the name of a B-list movie actor or someone from an Australian soap opera and she never would have noticed.

"Mr. Farnsley, sir, there's chocolate mousse for pudding, or we do still have the cake that was prepared for your father's birthday," Harold said as he began to clear plates from the table.

John frowned and then shook his head. "I don't think anyone wants pudding," he said sourly.

Speak for yourself, Janet thought, biting her tongue and keeping her eyes focussed on her empty plate. She knew that if she looked at Edward, he'd read her thoughts and make her laugh.

"Very good, sir," Harold said.

When the loud music started, it made everyone at the table jump. Joe grinned and got to his feet. "Sorry about that," he said as he pulled out his mobile. He glanced at the screen and then quickly walked out of the room.

"Shall we all move back into the sitting room and have another drink?" John asked.

"I think I'd rather go back to my room and try to get some sleep," Dawn said. "It's been a very long day."

"I'm going to need all of you together," Joe said as he stuck his head back through the doorway. "This is the solicitor in London, and he's telling me a lot of very interesting things."

"We'll be in the sitting room," John told him.

Joe nodded and then disappeared again. Everyone got up slowly. Janet waited until the last few people were leaving before she had a whispered conversation with Edward. Then they followed the others to the sitting room.

Sammy was back behind the bar, once again pouring wine. While Janet was tempted, she'd had a single glass of wine with dinner, and that was more than enough when she was working. Harold and Stuart walked into the room as everyone was taking seats.

"Did you need something?" John asked Harold.

"We were asked to join you here," Harold replied.

John nodded. "In that case, get a drink and have a seat."

Harold looked surprised for a moment before he simply sat in the nearest chair. Stuart shrugged and then walked to the bar. After a short conversation with Sammy, he was handed a drink. Then he sat down next to Harold.

"Sorry to have kept you waiting," Joe said when he walked into the silent room twenty minutes later.

Janet hadn't thought it possible, but the tension in the room seemed to increase as the man walked to its centre.

"Where should I start?" he asked.

"What did my father actually do with the trusts?" John demanded.

Joe grinned at him. "Not much," he replied.

"Not much? What does that mean?" Andrew asked.

"It means that he changed only one thing," Joe replied. "Obviously, I wasn't here, but you've all given me statements as to what Mr. Farnsley told you last night about the trusts. According to your father's primary solicitor, none of the changes that he discussed last night were ever made."

"So, he was planning to make them, but died before he could complete the process," John said.

"Not at all," Joe countered. "Apparently your father talked to all of his solicitors over the past few months and discussed various changes to the trusts with them. They were uniform in their opinion that your father could not legally make any of the changes he was suggesting."

"So, he wanted to make the changes, but wasn't allowed?" John asked.

"The solicitor with whom I spoke refused to go into any great detail as to what was actually discussed," Joe replied. "He insisted that whatever your father was proposing, nothing was actually done, so the proposals were irrelevant."

"I'm not certain that I would agree with that," John said.

"Perhaps, if the man in question is now going to be acting on your behalf, you'll have more success getting answers to that question than I did," Joe suggested.

John nodded. "Of course."

"But if none of it was true, why would Grandfather say such horrible things?" Stephanie asked.

"He was just winding you all up," Dawn told her. "He took great pleasure in that sort of thing. He used to lie in bed and pretend to be dead when we would go in to wake him in the mornings."

"And sometimes he'd look up symptoms of some disease in one of the medical books in the library in the house in London and then start insisting that he had that disease," Audrey added. "He very nearly had me convinced that he needed his gallbladder out until I discovered that it had already been taken out years ago."

Dawn nodded. "When I'd be standing over him, wondering if I should ring for an ambulance, he'd start to laugh and laugh."

"And that's what he would have done today," John said sadly. "When we all met for lunch, he'd have laughed at all of us for getting so upset last night."

"And he would have expected us to simply forgive him and move on," Margaret interjected. "But what he did last night was incredibly cruel, especially to Andrew."

Everyone around the table nodded.

"If he were still alive, I think I'd tell him to keep his money," Andrew said. "It wouldn't be easy, but Stephanie and I could survive without it."

"But now you don't have to," Margaret said brightly. "We're all right back where we started with piles of lovely money. Bigger piles now, because everything shifts, doesn't it?" she asked.

"Not exactly," Joe said.

"What does that mean?" John demanded.

"As I said, Mr. Farnsley did manage to make one change to the provisions of the trust, one that his solicitors think will stand up to any court battles," Joe told him.

"We'll see about that," John shot back. "What is the change?"

"The original trusts recognised only heirs born in wedlock. Mr. Farnsley told his solicitors that he felt that was an old-fashioned way of handling things and had the trusts changed so that they now recognise all children born in wedlock and assumed to be legal heirs, or any born outside of marriage who can prove their relationship to the family through DNA testing."

"So, Andrew is safe," Margaret said.

Joe nodded. "But if anyone comes forwards, claiming to be Mr. Arthur Farnsley's biological child, he or she can take a DNA test. If that DNA test proves the relationship, that child will be entitled to half of the income of the trusts, with the other half going to Mr. John Farnsley and his offspring in the same percentages as they do currently."

"Mr. Farnsley was my father," Dawn and Audrey both blurted out at the same moment.

Chapter 15

The room went silent for several seconds. Eventually, Dawn began to laugh.

"You should see all of your faces," she said. "I'm only teasing."

"I'm not," Audrey said flatly. "Mr. Farnsley was my father."

John cleared his throat. "I'm certain you appreciate that we'll need a DNA test to prove that."

"Of course," Audrey nodded.

"Do you have any evidence to back up your claim?" Edward asked.

"My mother was Mr. Farnsley's sixth wife," Audrey told him. "When he found out that she was pregnant, he threw her out. He told her that he didn't want any additional heirs to dilute his fortune. My mother was left homeless and alone in the world."

"How dreadful for her," Janet said.

Audrey nodded. "My bedtime stories weren't about princesses or fairies. They were all about the Farnsley family. My mother wanted me to know how badly she'd been treated so that I didn't make the same mistakes with my life."

"Why would you go to work for him, then?" Stephanie demanded.

Audrey hesitated and then shrugged. "I didn't know it was him when I was first offered the job. After my mother's death, when I was only ten, I did everything I could to put the past behind me. I studied hard and became a nurse and dedicated my life to helping people. I moved into private nursing because it allows me to have a more direct impact on my patients, letting me give them the best quality of life that I can for whatever time they have left."

"And then you were offered the job with the man you believed was your father. That must have been a shock," Janet suggested, watching Audrey very closely.

"It was a shock, but I was happy to do it. Happy isn't the right word. I was resigned to doing it. I was paid well, and for a few brief months, I had an opportunity to actually get to know the man who'd been so horrible to my mother," Audrey replied.

"You must have hated him," Janet said.

"I, er, I soon came to pity him. With all of his wealth and power, he'd done nothing with his life. The only thing that amused him in his old age was pretending to be dead to upset his nurses. He was a sad and rather pathetic person in the end."

"When did you tell him that you are his daughter?" Janet asked.

Audrey shook her head. "I didn't."

"This must have seemed the perfect place to tell him. There weren't many people around, and you could have his undivided attention, especially after the big family argument. He must have been in a wonderful mood, too, knowing that he'd upset everyone," Janet said thoughtfully. "What did he say when you told him?"

"I didn't tell him," Audrey insisted.

"He probably laughed," Janet guessed. "And he probably insisted that you weren't his daughter. He probably told you that your mother had had an affair and deserved to be thrown out of his house. You probably thought he was only winding you up, though, teasing you before he was going to accept you as his own."

"He was lying," Audrey said through tears. "He lied to me and told me that my mother was a whore and that she didn't even know who my father had been. He lied and said that he'd given her money every month for the first year of my life, but that he'd stopped helping her when he discovered that she'd used it all for a holiday for herself and a lover instead of spending it on me."

"You must have been very angry," Janet said softly.

"He lied and lied and lied until I couldn't even think straight," Audrey told her. "And he expected me to just stand there and take it. I was sobbing and begging him to stop, but he just kept going on and on about how I knew nothing and how my mother couldn't be trusted. He tried to destroy my memories of the most wonderful, sweet, beautiful woman, but I wouldn't let him do it."

"So you killed him," Janet concluded.

A few people gasped, but Audrey just nodded. "It was self-defense," she said calmly. "His words were destroying me. I had to make him stop. I had no choice."

"I'll take it from here," Joe said as he put a hand on Audrey's arm.

"I don't want my share of his money," Audrey said as she stood up. "You can keep the money, but I do want to be acknowledged as his daughter. He would hate that."

"Let's see what the DNA test reveals," John said.

"It will reveal the ugly truth, and if you deny it again, I'll sue you for every penny I can get from your stupid trust funds," Audrey shouted at him. "That man, that horrible, evil, nasty man was my father, and there's nothing you can do or say to change that fact."

"Let's get you over to Nassau," Joe said. "We'll worry about everything else tomorrow."

"It was self-defense," Audrey was still insisting as Joe led her out of the room.

Edward got up and followed the pair. Everyone sat in silence until he returned a short while later.

"She's going to need to be hospitalised," Dawn said. "She's not fit to stand trial."

"She murdered my father," John snapped.

"She also thought he was her father," Stephanie interjected. "That's all sorts of messed up."

"He'd had a vasectomy," John said.

"Before or after his sixth marriage?" Rachel asked.

"Before. He had it before his second marriage, actually. He waited quite a few years after my mother died before he married again, and before he did, he made certain that he wasn't going to have any additional children," John replied.

"So it seems highly unlikely that he's actually Audrey's father," Andrew said.

"I'd call it impossible," John replied. "But we can wait for the DNA test results to be certain."

"And on that note, I suggest we all get some sleep," Edward said. "It's not that late, but it's been a horribly long day."

"And yesterday was terribly difficult as well," John added as everyone began to get up from their seats. "Let's hope tomorrow will be a better day."

"There will be a number of police and other security

personnel on the island tonight," John told them. "With the murderer behind bars, though, I suspect they'll all be withdrawn tomorrow."

As the grandchildren and their spouses began to leave the room, Edward caught Janet's hand. "Wait," he mouthed at her.

She sighed and then dropped her handbag. As she reached down to pick it up, the last of the younger couples left the room.

"Do you need anything else for now?" Harold asked John.

"No, all three of you can go to bed, or go and get drunk, or whatever you want to do," John told him. "I'm going to have a drink with my old school friend, as I'm fairly certain he's going to want to get off the island as soon as the police say he can go."

"I'm ready to leave now," Janet announced.

"Tomorrow," Edward told her. "Assuming the inspector agrees."

"Scotch," John said. "I have a wonderful new single malt that I just discovered."

"I'm going to bed," Sarah announced before she swept out of the room.

"Perhaps I should stay and pour for you," Sammy suggested.

"Yes, indeed," John said. He and Edward walked to the bar with Sammy. Janet stood by her chair, wondering what to do.

"I can escort you back to your cottage," Harold offered. "Or take you in the golf cart, if you'd prefer."

Before Janet could reply, the two men at the bar laughed uproariously. As Janet looked over, they both emptied their glasses and put them back on the bar.

"More of the same, or do you want to try something else?" John asked.

"More of the same," Edward replied.

"I think I'd better stay and keep an eye on my husband," Janet told Harold. She scowled and then watched as Harold and Stuart left the room.

John and Edward were putting their empty glasses back on the bar again when she reached them.

"I think that's quite enough," she said sharply.

"Don't listen to her," John said. "We're only just getting started."

"Do you remember the time when Shorty and Blazes found a way into the kitchen after hours and stole all of the cooking wine?" Edward asked.

John laughed. "And then they sold the bottles to the rest of us for far more than they were worth."

"And we all got drunk and sick everywhere."

Janet stood and stared at Edward for the next half hour while he and John drank continuously and reminisced about all of their schoolboy adventures. They nearly all seemed to involve too much alcohol, but Janet couldn't be certain if any of them were true or not. *Was it possible that Edward had gone to school with John? If he hadn't, John had to know who they were and must have been playing along.* After a while, Sammy began to seem nervous.

"I think this has gone on for long enough," Janet said.

Sammy looked relieved. "Mr. Farnsley, do you still need me?" he asked.

John frowned. "I suppose not. You go and get some sleep. I can pour my own Scotch."

"We should go," Janet said firmly.

"Okay," Edward said.

He took a step towards the door and then staggered

sideways. His next attempt sent him stumbling in the other direction. Janet frowned and then took his arm.

"Let's go," she said sharply.

"I think I'm in trouble," Edward called over his shoulder, waving to John and Sammy as Janet pulled him out of the room.

They walked down the corridor to the front door. As Janet opened the door, Edward began to sing badly.

"Do stop," Janet said.

"It's a beautiful night. I'm on a beautiful island with a beautiful woman. Life doesn't get better than this," he argued before he started singing again, more loudly.

"Edward, a man died here today," she reminded him. "Please behave appropriately."

Edward frowned and then nodded slowly. "You're right, of course. I'll sing quietly."

"If you sing one more note, I'm leaving you," Janet said loudly.

They'd made their way from the house down to the road. As they began the slow descent to the beach, Edward stopped and then staggered sideways behind a small cluster of palm trees, dragging Janet along with him.

"I think we're out of sight here," he whispered in her ear.

"Now what?"

"Now we go to work," he replied. "Ideally, we'll get to the waterfall without being seen, but if anyone spots us, I'm drunk and you're furious."

"Why aren't you drunk? You drank half a bottle of Scotch."

"Later."

Edward set off at a brisk pace, walking along the sand next to the road. It was dark enough to make the walking difficult, but Janet felt as if they were far too visible by the light of the half-full moon. They walked in silence for several minutes before they heard the sound of an engine.

Another small grouping of palm trees gave them a place to hide as the golf cart drove past them.

"Sammy," Edward said in a low voice.

Janet nodded.

"And he didn't go far," Edward added as the sound of the engine stopped.

As they resumed walking along the road, Janet realised that she could hear a waterfall somewhere nearby. Hoping that the sound would help cover their movements, she began to walk even faster. Just a moment or two later, Edward grabbed her arm and pulled her sideways, off the road and into the sand. They crept sideways and then forwards until they could see the golf cart parked where the road seemed to end. From what Janet could see, Sammy was still sitting in the driver's seat.

Edward sighed softly and then crouched down on the sand. He slowly pulled himself forwards, inching towards the parked cart. Not knowing what else to do, Janet followed suit, frowning as she wiggled her way through the thick sand. When they got close enough, Janet could see that Sammy was on his mobile phone.

"...more minutes and then I'm out of here," Sammy said before he threw the phone onto the passenger seat.

How many more minutes? Janet wondered. *Five, ten, fifteen?*

She was still wondering when she heard the sound of another motor. She looked down the road, but couldn't see anyone coming. Edward tapped her arm and then gestured towards the water. A large boat was approaching. It stopped some distance away from the shore, and Janet watched as a smaller boat was lowered from the larger boat's deck. A moment later, someone began rowing the smaller boat towards the beach that Janet could see below them.

"What took you so long?" Sammy demanded as Joe climbed up the path from the beach to the road. Joe got into the cart, leaving the door ajar, which meant the interior light stayed on, giving Janet and Edward a clear view of the pair.

"I was booking someone for murder," Joe replied. "You wouldn't believe how much paperwork that creates."

"At least the case is solved and the family can leave the island," Sammy replied.

"Yeah. Tomorrow I'll tell them the rest of the story."

"There's more?"

Joe laughed. "Old man Farnsley wasn't stupid. He kept things friendly between himself and his former wives, not just the ones who fell pregnant, but all of them. And he left complete records of everything he did with his solicitors."

"So he was telling Audrey the truth about her mother?"

"He was. He sent her away when she told him she was pregnant, but he paid for her to live very comfortably until the baby was born. Then he provided a generous sum each month so that she could provide for the baby."

"And she blew it all on a holiday?"

Joe laughed. "And while she was off partying with some other man, Arthur had a blood test done on the baby. It proved beyond a shadow of a doubt that he wasn't Audrey's father. When the ex-wife got home from her holiday, he cut her off without a penny."

"Harsh on the baby."

"If she'd saved the money he'd given her since they'd divorced, she'd have been able to live modestly for years. Instead, she'd spent it all on herself, expecting Arthur to keep supporting her, even though she'd cheated on him.

I've no doubt she was bitter and angry when he finally cut her off, but I don't blame him for doing so."

"Whatever," Sammy snapped. "We need to talk about the next shipment."

"What about it?"

"I want forty per cent this time."

Joe sighed. "We've been through this before. You get thirty per cent and you should consider yourself lucky."

"After all the scrambling I had to do to rearrange things because the family suddenly decided to visit this weekend, I want more."

"Scrambling you had to do?" Joe echoed. "Do you have any idea what I've been through this week? I'm being watched more closely than ever before. This is going to be my last run."

"You can't be serious. We're doing great."

"But people are getting suspicious."

Sammy laughed. "Don't start telling me about that top-secret government agency again, the one that you sort of work with, but not really, but kinda. I don't believe a word of it."

"It's all true."

"Yeah, and Edward and Janet Thomas-Blanchard are agents," Sammy said. "Have you spent any time with them at all? She's a spoiled bitch who can't wait to get out of here, and he's one of John's old school friends. He drank over half a bottle of Scotch tonight and then stumbled out of the house on his wife's arm while she shouted at him for getting drunk and behaving badly."

Joe grinned. "I said they were agents. I didn't say they were very good at their job. From what I could ascertain, Edward used to be an agent, but he was asked to retire because he'd developed a drinking problem. Janet is some dumb secretary from the agency's typing pool, but they sent her along to keep an eye on him. Clearly, she's not doing a good job of it."

"You can tell me whatever you like, but I won't believe they're anything other than what they claim to be. Stupid rich folks who are simply getting in the way of my little venture."

"Our little venture," Joe corrected him. "Don't forget that we're partners in this venture."

"Not equal partners, though, are we?"

"I've explained all of this before. You get thirty per cent and I get thirty per cent. I use the rest to pay the boat captains and to bribe everyone that has to bribed along the way."

"Maybe you should get rid of a few of the people you need to bribe."

"Are you suggesting that I start killing people?"

Sammy shrugged. "I want forty per cent. I don't really care how you make that happen, but you make it happen or you find a new drop location."

"The next shipment is due on Tuesday. I can't find another drop location that quickly."

"So, stop paying Jackson or Donahue and we'll both get more."

"I'll think about it."

"You do that."

Joe sat and stared at Sammy for a short while before he slowly got out of the cart. "I could just arrest you," he said softly. "And then make new arrangements with whoever replaces you."

"I have recordings of every conversation we've ever had tucked away somewhere safe," Sammy replied. "And someone who you don't even know exists knows exactly where to find them and what to do with them if anything ever happens to me."

After a minute, Joe turned and walked back down the path to the beach below. Janet watched as he rowed his way back to the larger boat. It wasn't until the larger boat was motoring away that Sammy started the engine on the golf cart and drove away.

Janet and Edward stayed where they were on the sand for several additional minutes before Edward finally stood up and helped Janet to her feet. As they began to walk back down the road, Edward started sending text messages.

"So, Sammy and Joe are running a drug smuggling operation from this island when the family isn't here?" Janet asked as they walked.

"It certainly sounds that way," Edward replied. "But we'll be long gone by Tuesday when their next shipment gets interrupted."

"As much as I'd like to be here to see that, I'm ready to get out of here," Janet told him.

As they approached their cottage, Edward began to sing again. Janet frowned and then stormed away from him, stopping short when she spotted the security guard behind their cottage. Edward smiled widely at the man as they walked past him.

"I have sand everywhere," he announced loudly as he opened their cottage door. "I'm sorry I fell over, and I'm sorry I pulled you down with me."

"I wouldn't have minded so much if you hadn't refused to get up for the last hour," Janet countered as she pushed the door shut behind them.

THREE DAYS LATER, Janet opened her eyes and sighed happily. "There's no place like home," she told Edward as he rolled towards her.

"And not a grain of sand in sight," he replied as he pulled her into a kiss. "I never appreciated how wonderful it is that Doveby Dale isn't near the sea."

"I'm still washing sand out of my hair."

Edward's phone buzzed before he could reply. He grabbed the device and then smiled.

"What's happened?"

"Sammy and Joe were arrested last night. That's good news, but even better, the agency was able to track down the two men who were mentioned as being bribed as part of the scheme. Both of them have been charged, and one of them has been talking, a lot."

"Excellent," Janet said. "It was almost worth lying in the sand for six hours for that."

"It wasn't six hours."

"It felt as if it were six hours."

"Audrey is being sent to a mental hospital in the UK. The results from the DNA test she took are still pending, but Mr. Jones was able to verify that Audrey and Arthur had incompatible blood types. There's no way he was her father."

"I hope they won't tell her that until she's under treatment."

They snuggled together under the duvet.

"So, Smith was concerned about the drug smuggling, not the murder," Janet said.

"It seems so. I gather that Joe had done a few things that had raised a few question marks, so Smith no longer trusted him. I don't think Smith or anyone else actually thought he was running a drug smuggling ring. I suspect the agency simply thought Joe was being bribed to ignore what was happening in the area."

"I don't understand why we couldn't be told why we were being sent, though."

Edward shrugged. "I suspect Smith was less concerned about Joe than he was about protecting someone on the island. I'm just not certain who we were there to protect."

Edward's phone rang a moment later. "It's Mr. Jones."

"I'm not ready for another assignment."

Edward chuckled. "That makes two of us. Hello?" he said as he pushed the button to put the call on speaker.

"Ah, good morning. Are you and Janet both there?"

"Yes. You're on speaker," Edward told him.

"Excellent. Hold, please," Mr. Jones said.

Janet and Edward exchanged glances.

"Janet, Edward, very good work," another voice said. "I'm very impressed with both of you. We'll be in touch."

"Who was that?" Janet demanded as the phone went dead.

Edward stared at her for a moment before he replied. "I'm going to guess it was Smith," he said, sounding as if he didn't quite believe his own words.

"It was a woman's voice."

"I thought it was a man's," Edward countered.

He flopped back on his pillow and stared at the ceiling. "I worked for the agency for over forty years," he said. "In all those years, Smith never rang me, not once."

"He or she rang you today."

"He or she rang you today," he countered. "You've been working for the agency for less than six months, and you've already been congratulated by Smith."

"We've been congratulated by Smith," she told him. "We're a team. Remember that."

He sighed and then pulled her close. "We're a team," he repeated. "And I've never been happier."

The George Assignment
A JANET MARKHAM BENNETT COZY THRILLER

Release date: September 16, 2022

Janet and Edward are enjoying life in Doveby Dale, planning their carriage house remodel, when Mr. Jones arrives with a new and rather urgent assignment. Another agent has disappeared. While there are any number of possible explanations for the disappearance, none of them are good.

As Janet and Edward follow the missing man's trail from Edinburgh to Paris to Berlin, it begins to seem as if he's disappeared by choice, which raises a number of other worrying possibilities.

Has the agent been taken or has he disappeared voluntarily? Are Janet and Edward walking into a trap? And is this going to be their most dangerous assignment yet?

A sneak peek at The George Assignment

A Janet Markham Bennett Cozy Thriller
Release date: September 16, 2022

Please excuse any typos or minor errors. I have not yet completed final edits on this title.

Chapter One

"This is going to be amazing when it's finished," Charlie Mathison said.

"I hope so," Joan Markham Donaldson replied. "We're spending a great deal of money on this project."

Charlie nodded. "But you want the best of everything."

"Some of us do, anyway," Joan muttered as she glanced sideways at her sister.

"The some of us who will be living in the space," Janet Markham Bennett replied. "And we're also the one who will be paying for it all," she reminded her sister.

Joan nodded. "The end result will be nicer than Doveby House."

Janet laughed. "There's no way our little carriage house conversion will ever be nicer than Doveby House. You can't compare a seventeenth century manor house with multiple bedrooms, a conservatory, and a library to what we're doing out here."

"You've managed to squeeze quite a lot into a fairly small space," Charlie said. "Adding the loft doubled your space."

"It should give us a bit more space than what we currently have, anyway," Janet replied.

"Where are you now?" Charlie asked.

"In the largest of the first floor bedrooms," Janet told him.

He nodded. "I did a lot of the work in Doveby House when Margaret Appleton owned it," he explained. "Maggie rang me when she first bought the house and we worked together on reconfiguring the entire first floor. When she bought it, there were seven or eight tiny bedrooms up there an not a single loo."

"Did Ms. Appleton buy the property intending to turn it into a bed and breakfast, then?" Janet wondered.

"She did. Originally she wanted four bedrooms upstairs, but she wanted them all to be en suite and she wanted them to be large enough to be comfortable, so we ended up doing three and then her large suite on the ground floor," Charlie explained.

"And the kitchen extension," Janet added.

"I didn't do the kitchen or the bathrooms, for that matter. I don't do a lot of plumbing or electrical work. I'll get your walls and loft built here and then work with the people you've chosen to do the kitchen and bathroom," he replied.

"How long do you think it will take to do the entire project?" Joan asked.

Charlie shrugged. "Assuming I don't run into any issues, three or four months, maybe."

Janet frowned. "So you won't be finished until September or October?"

"Let's say November to be on the safe side," Charlie replied.

"You may be travelling for some of that time," Joan said encouragingly.

Janet swallowed a sigh. Joan was correct. She and Edward might be travelling. And if they didn't need to travel, they could still choose to travel.

"I wish I'd known that Maggie was going to sell Doveby House," Charlie said as he began another slow stroll around the carriage house. "I might have put in an offer."

"She passed away unexpectedly and left the property to a local charity," Janet told him. "They were eager to sell it as quickly as possible. They didn't have any use for a bed and breakfast."

"I hope I'm not being rude if I ask why you bought it," Charlie said. "No offense, but I'm hoping to be retired when I get to your age."

Janet felt herself blushing as she bit her tongue. She looked at her sister and saw that Joan hadn't taken the comment well, either. To be fair, they were both retired, but it was never nice to be reminded of ones age.

"We are both retired," Janet told him after an awkward pause. "We both taught primary school for decades."

"What about your husbands? Are they both retired, too?" Charlie asked.

Janet grinned. "They are both retired, but we'd never met either of them before we bought Doveby House."

Charlie stared at her for a moment and then scratched his head. "So why did you buy Doveby House?"

"Owning a bed and breakfast was always a dream of mine," Joan told him. "That's all it was, though. A dream. I never had the resources needed to buy a property large enough to use as a bed and breakfast. Janet and I both trained as teachers and when she finished her training, we bought a little cottage together. We lived there, sharing the cottage and a car, throughout our working lives. When I was ready to retired, we determined that Janet could also afford to retire. Our plan was to live simply and travel whenever we had the opportunity."

Janet laughed. "It sounds such a simple plan," she said. "And yet here we are, living incredibly complicated lives."

"So what happened?" Charlie demanded.

"We were fortune enough to unexpectedly inherit some money from a distant relative," Janet told him. "And while I was busy mentally planning trips around the world, Joan found the particulars for Doveby House in an estate agent's window."

"It was almost exactly what I'd always pictured when I'd thought about having a bed and breakfast," Joan took up the story. "I persuaded Janet to come with me to see the property, and we both fell in love."

"It's a beautiful old house. I loved working on it," Charlie said.

"You did excellent work," Janet told him. "As soon as we'd seen the entire property, we made an offer."

"And, to our surprise, the offer was accepted," Joan added. "The sale included all of the furniture and everything in the house, so we were able to sell our cottage and move in almost immediately."

"And then you reopened the bed and breakfast,"

Charlie said. "But how did you meet your husbands? Were they both guests?"

"Michael, Joan's husband, lived across the street," Janet told him.

Charlie raised an eyebrow. "In the house that burned down?"

"Actually, he lived in the half of the semi-detached property that is still standing," Joan told him.

"Still standing, but not entirely habitable," Janet added.

"I know the builders who are rebuilding the missing half," Charlie told them. "They said that side was completely destroyed."

"It was," Janet agreed.

"I feel sorry for whoever lived there," Charlie added. "Didn't I hear that the fire was started deliberately?"

"I don't believe that that has been proven in court yet," Joan told him. "But one of the home's former occupants is awaiting trial on that charge."

"And here's Stuart," Janet said loudly as she spotted the man walking towards the carriage house.

"Stuart owned the house that burned down," Joan told Charlie in a low voice.

"Good morning," Stuart said brightly as he walked into the carriage house. He looked around and then shook his head. "I still can't get over how large the space in here actually is. It never seemed this large when it was full of boxes and stuff."

"Maggie used to for storage," Charlie said. "We moved nearly everything out of the main house and into here while we were redoing the interior. I suspect very little of what was in the house when Maggie bought it actually ever made it back into the house."

"There wasn't a lot of furniture in here," Janet said.

"No, there wasn't a lot of furniture in the house,"

A sneak peek at The George Assignment

Charlie told her. "Just about every room was full of boxes. Maggie opened a few, now and then, but most of them seemed to be full of piles of papers. I don't know why anyone would keep their electricity bills for twenty years, but apparently, some people do. There were a lot of books, too, but most were water-damaged and old. Maggie just had me bring everything out here and stack it as neatly as possible. It wasn't easy, though, because the gardens were overgrown back then."

Stuart nodded. "That was before I moved in. I remember telling Mary as we were moving in that I wanted to have a word with whoever owned Doveby House as soon as we were settled. It was obvious that the gardens had once been beautiful, but they'd been terribly neglected for years."

Janet looked out through the carriage house doors at the stunning gardens that surrounded them. "I can't imagine."

"It took me years to bring them back to their former glory," Stuart said. "It was a labour of love, of course, even if Mary did complain constantly about it."

Since Mary had subsequently drugged Stuart and then set their house on fire, complaining didn't seem so bad to Janet.

"And you've done an amazing job of keeping the gardens beautiful ever since," Joan told him.

Stuart flushed. "You know I love it." He looked at Charlie. "I was a gardener my entire life." He named the stately home where he'd once been head gardener. "Officially, I'm retired, but I still love nothing more than spending a few hours each day digging in the soil, planting, and weeding."

"And I complain when I have to cut the grass," Charlie laughed.

"Actually, cutting grass is one of my least favourite jobs," Stuart told him.

Janet tuned them out as the two men began to discuss the job, one that she'd never done. When she and Joan had lived in their little cottage, they'd paid a neighbour to cut their small patch of grass when he did his. Over the decades, the neighbours had changed and the price had risen, but Janet and Joan had always managed to avoid the chore.

They were still talking five minutes later, when Stuart's mobile rang. He jumped and then pulled out the device.

"Hello?"

"Hi, Teresa."

"I'll see you, then." Stuart dropped his phone back into his pocket as he blushed. He looked a Janet and then Joan. "Um, that was Teresa," he said. He glanced at Charlie. "She used to teach with Janet and Joan," he explained.

"And she came to stay with us a few months ago," Joan explained.

"And she and Stuart became friends," Janet added, hiding a grin as Stuart blushed even more brightly.

"She's coming to visit again," Stuart said.

Joan nodded. "She told me that she will be here around five."

"That's what she told me, too," Stuart agreed. "We're going to have dinner at that little French restaurant tonight."

"Oh, very nice," Janet said. The French restaurant was the fanciest restaurant in Doveby Dale and the surrounding area. It was where Edward had taken her the first time they'd gone out.

Stuart shrugged. "After everything that happened with

Mary, I didn't think I'd ever want to fall in love again, but Teresa is very special."

"You do know that she's been married seven times before, don't you?" Joan asked.

"Oh, she's told me all about all of her husbands," Stuart replied. "And I've told her all about my wives, especially Mary. I reckon if she's had seven husbands and none of them have ever tried to kill her, that she's doing better than I am."

Janet chuckled. "You may be right about that."

"Are you definitely having the carriage house converted into a self-catering unit, then?" Stuart asked Joan.

"We're having it converted into a small flat," Joan replied. "Janet and Edward are going to be moving out here once it's finished."

"That makes sense," Stuart replied. "And now I should get on with some weeding and watering. It's been very dry for June."

He turned and walked away, leaving the sisters with Charlie.

"You were telling me how you met your husbands," Charlie said.

"My husband, Michael, lived across the road," Joan reminded him.

"Michael Donaldson? The chemist?" Charlie replied.

Joan nodded.

"I didn't realise he lived here, and I didn't realise that he'd remarried. Everyone in Doveby Dale knew him when he had his shop in the village. I suppose I knew that he lived in the area somewhere, but I never really thought about where."

"He still owns the house across the street," Janet told him.

"It probably still smells of smoke," Charlie guessed.

"Was there any water damage?"

"None, but it does still smell of smoke," Joan agreed. "We've taken out all of the furniture, had new carpets fitted, changed the curtains, and painted every inch of every room, and it still smells of smoke."

"It should improve over time," Charlie assured her. "And once they truly get started on rebuilding the other half of the semi, you'll get even more paint and carpeting smells."

"Fortunately, we've plenty of room in Doveby House," Joan said.

"Maggie made certain that her suite was large and comfortable," Charlie said with a laugh. "She said that if she had to cook and clean for demanding guests all day long, she needed an oasis to go back to every night. She also wanted enough space to entertain overnight guests from time to time."

"Yes, well, now Michael and I are enjoying having all of that space," Joan said.

"You didn't know Michael before you moved to Doveby Dale?" Charlie asked.

"No, we met him when we went across the road to introduce ourselves to our new neighbours," Joan explained.

And then he asked Joan to have dinner with him and she was too shocked to reply, Janet thought. *Fortunately, I said yes on her behalf.*

"How long have you been married?" Charlie asked.

"He asked me to marry him last Valentine's Day and we just celebrated our first wedding anniversary last week," Joan told him.

"Congratulations," Charlie said.

"Thank you," Joan replied.

Charlie looked at Janet. "So how did you meet your

husband?" he asked her.

"Edward was our first guest," Janet explained. "When he arrived, he told us that he had made a booking with Margaret Appleton."

Charlie nodded. "That probably happened a lot when you first bought the property, didn't it? I know Maggie was generally very busy."

"Actually, Edward was the only one," Janet said. *And he didn't really have a previous booking, either,* she thought. But she wasn't about to tell Charlie the true story.

"And then he swept you off your feet?" Charlie teased.

"He did, rather," Janet replied. He'd been charming and sweet, but also mysterious and annoying. Before he'd left, he'd explained to her that he'd been sent to Doveby House because he worked for a secret government agency that had occasionally used the property as a safe house. He was there to make sure that Maggie Appleton hadn't left behind any evidence of a connection between the house and his agency.

While Janet had still been trying to process all of that, Edward had added that he was attracted to her and interested in getting to know her better. Unfortunately, while he was supposed to be retired, he was still being sent on assignments all around the world. When he'd left, he'd promised to stay in touch, but that had never been easy.

"Presumably, he wasn't here for long," Charlie said.

"He wasn't here for long," Janet agreed. "He was meant to be retired, but he was still travelling a great deal for work. That meant he couldn't get back to Doveby Dale very often."

"Did he shower you with flowers and ring you nightly?" Charlie asked. "That's what I did when I was in a long-distance relationship. She still found someone else, though."

"I'm sorry," Janet replied. "And yes, he did send flowers, and gifts as well, and he rang me when he could."

"Gifts? Maybe that's where I went wrong," Charlie laughed. "What did he send you?"

"A painting that I'd admired in a local shop, a kitten, and a car," Janet replied.

Charlie's jaw dropped. "A car? He really was serious, wasn't he? Tell me it was a really expensive brand new car."

Janet laughed. "It was a reasonably priced secondhand car," she told him. "But it was the first car that I'd ever owned that I didn't have to share with Joan."

"First?" Joan asked.

Janet laughed. "Only," she said. "It's the little red car in the car park outside."

Charlie nodded. "I saw it when I parked. It suits you."

"Thanks." Janet felt oddly pleased by the comment.

"So after all of those gifts, you had to marry him," Charlie suggested.

Janet laughed. "Not at all, but eventually, after Joan's wedding, Edward finally actually retired properly." *Mostly*, she thought.

"And then he came to stay here so that he could court Janet properly," Joan added.

"How long have you been married, then?" Charlie wondered.

"We got married just after Christmas," Janet told him. "And the last six months have been a complete whirlwind of adventure."

"Adventure?" Charlie echoed.

Janet flushed. "Edward was very successful in his chosen career. He owns properties all around the world. Since we've been married, we've been travelling more than we've been here."

A sneak peek at The George Assignment

All of that was true, even if Janet had left out one piece of information

"Where have you been?" Charlie asked.

"London, Edinburgh, central Florida, New York City, and the Bahamas," Janet replied.

"All of that in six months? Why are you bothering with the conversion here, then? If I could travel that much, I'd never be at home," Charlie said.

"We love to travel, but we also love coming back to Doveby House," Janet explained. "But as much as we love Doveby House, Edward and I would both prefer to have our own space, away from the guests."

Charlie laughed. "I can totally understand that. I can't imagine living with total strangers in the next room. Staying in a hotel is bad enough. I couldn't have strangers in my home."

"I'm sorry I'm late," Edward said as he walked into the carriage house.

Janet felt her heart flutter as she looked at the handsome man. There was still a part of her that couldn't quite believe that he was her husband.

He crossed to her and kissed her cheek. "Have you gone over the plans yet?" he asked.

Charlie nodded. "It's going to be amazing when it's done," he said.

"Yes, we think so," Edward replied. "We're looking forward..."

Edward's mobile began to buzz loudly. As he reached for it, Janet's went off, as well, filling the air with a cacophony of sound. As Janet dug into her handbag to find her phone, she realised that not all of the noise was coming from inside the carriage house. Loud sirens seemed to be going off somewhere outside.

"What's happening?" Joan asked as they all looked towards the door.

Janet worried momentarily about the carriage house ghost who had a bad habit of locking people inside of the building. Apparently, the ghost was able to recognise an emergency when it happened, as the door remained open as they ran towards it.

Outside, they all stopped and stared at the row of police cars that seemed to be racing towards Doveby House. Janet found her mobile and dug it out. She frowned at the screen and then looked at Edward. He held up his phone so that she could see the same message on his that she'd read on hers.

URGENT ASSIGNMENT! ON OUR WAY! was all that it said.

Janet watched as the first of the police cars screeched to a halt in front of Doveby House. Behind the third car was a black limousine. Janet didn't bother to count the number of police cars behind the limousine.

Edward looked at Janet. "We have company," he said softly.

"They're here for you?" Charlie asked. "What did you do? I mean, should I forget about this job or what? That's a lot of police for just one person."

Edward grinned at him.. "I'm one of the good guys," he assured him. "You get started on the carriage house. I have a feeling Janet and I may need to go away for a few days, though."

He didn't wait for a reply. Instead, he took Janet's arm and the pair began a hurried walk towards the car park. They were only halfway there when Mr. Jones emerged from the limousine.

The Body in the Annex

Now available to pre-order – the first book in Diana's new series:

The Body in the Annex
A Sunset Lodge Mystery

Release date: July 28, 2022.

After months of planning, sisters Abigail and Amanda Clark have finally purchased a historic resort property in the Finger Lakes. Abigail has years of experience managing hotels and restaurants, so she's sure she's ready for this new challenge. She isn't even bothered when her sister takes her dream job and decides not to move to Nightshade right away.

When a guest turns up dead in one of the rooms, though, Abigail finds herself caught up in the middle of a murder investigation. That definitely wasn't in her plans.

The dead man had a lot of enemies in the small town of Nightshade, New York, and it isn't long before Abigail has met several of them. Her nosy neighbor is eager to poke her nose into the police investigation, but all Abigail wants to do is find some guests for Sunset Lodge.

Can Abigail fix up the historic hotel on a shoestring budget? Will she be able to find guests who don't mind that a man was murdered in the hotel's annex? Or will Abigail's neighbor say the wrong thing to the wrong person and get someone else murdered before the police find the killer?

Also by Diana Xarissa

The Janet Markham Bennett Cozy Thrillers

The Armstrong Assignment
The Blake Assignment
The Carlson Assignment
The Doyle Assignment
The Everest Assignment
The Farnsley Assignment
The George Assignment

The Markham Sisters Cozy Mystery Novellas

The Appleton Case
The Bennett Case
The Chalmers Case
The Donaldson Case
The Ellsworth Case
The Fenton Case
The Green Case
The Hampton Case
The Irwin Case
The Jackson Case
The Kingston Case
The Lawley Case

The Moody Case

The Norman Case

The Osborne Case

The Patrone Case

The Quinton Case

The Rhodes Case

The Somerset Case

The Tanner Case

The Underwood Case

The Vernon Case

The Walters Case

The Xanders Case

The Young Case

The Zachery Case

The Isle of Man Ghostly Cozy Mysteries

Arrivals and Arrests

Boats and Bad Guys

Cars and Cold Cases

Dogs and Danger

Encounters and Enemies

Friends and Frauds

Guests and Guilt

Hop-tu-Naa and Homicide

Invitations and Investigations

Joy and Jealousy

Kittens and Killers

Letters and Lawsuits

Marsupials and Murder

Neighbors and Nightmares

Orchestras and Obsessions

Proposals and Poison

Questions and Quarrels

Roses and Revenge

Secrets and Suspects

Theaters and Threats

Umbrellas and Undertakers

Visitors and Victims

Weddings and Witnesses

The Isle of Man Cozy Mysteries

Aunt Bessie Assumes

Aunt Bessie Believes

Aunt Bessie Considers

Aunt Bessie Decides

Aunt Bessie Enjoys

Aunt Bessie Finds

Aunt Bessie Goes

Aunt Bessie's Holiday

Aunt Bessie Invites

Aunt Bessie Joins

Aunt Bessie Knows

Aunt Bessie Likes

Aunt Bessie Meets

Aunt Bessie Needs

Aunt Bessie Observes

Aunt Bessie Provides

Aunt Bessie Questions

Aunt Bessie Remembers

Aunt Bessie Solves

Aunt Bessie Tries

Aunt Bessie Understands

Aunt Bessie Volunteers

Aunt Bessie Wonders

Aunt Bessie's X-Ray

Aunt Bessie Yearns

Aunt Bessie Zeroes In

The Aunt Bessie Cold Case Mysteries

The Adams File

The Bernhard File

The Carter File

The Durand File

The Evans File

The Flowers File

The Goodman File

The Sunset Lodge Mysteries

The Body in the Annex

The Isle of Man Romances

Island Escape

Island Inheritance

Island Heritage

Island Christmas

The Later in Life Love Stories

Second Chances

Second Act

Second Thoughts

Second Degree

Second Best

Second Nature

Second Place

Bookplates Are Now Available

Would you like a signed bookplate for this book?

I now have bookplates (stickers) that I can personalize, sign, and send to you. It's the next best thing to getting a signed copy!

Send an email to diana@dianaxarissa.com with your mailing address (I promise not to use it for anything else, ever) and how you'd like your bookplate personalized and I'll sign one and send it to you.

There is no charge for a bookplate, but there is a limit of one per person.

About the Author

Diana has been self-publishing since 2013, and she feels surprised and delighted to have found readers who enjoy the stories and characters that she imagines. Always an avid reader, she still loves nothing more than getting lost in fictional worlds, her own or others!

After being raised in Erie, Pennsylvania, and studying history at Allegheny College in Meadville, Pennsylvania, Diana pursued a career in college administration. She was living and working in Washington, DC, when she met her future husband, an Englishman who was visiting the city.

Following her marriage, Diana moved to Derbyshire. A short while later, she and her husband relocated to the Isle of Man. After ten years on the island, during which Diana earned a Master's degree in the island's history, they made the decision to relocate again, this time to the US.

Now living near Buffalo, New York, Diana and her husband live with their daughter, a student at the University at Buffalo. Their son is now living and working just outside of Boston, Massachusetts, giving Diana an excuse to travel now and again.

Diana also writes mystery/thrillers set in the not-too-distant future as Diana X. Dunn and Young Adult fiction as D.X. Dunn.

She is always happy to hear from readers. You can write to her at:

Diana Xarissa Dunn
PO Box 72
Clarence, NY 14031.

Find Diana at: DianaXarissa.com
E-mail: Diana@dianaxarissa.com

Printed in Great Britain
by Amazon